A DREAM OF WHITE HORSES

A DREAM OF WHITE HORSES

By

Paul Scraton

Bluemoose

Copyright © Paul Scraton 2024

First published in 2024 by
Bluemoose Books Ltd
25 Sackville Street
Hebden Bridge
West Yorkshire
HX7 7DJ

www.bluemoosebooks.com

British Library Cataloguing-in-Publication data
A catalogue record for this book is available from the British Library

Paperback
ISBN 978 1 915693 20 4

Printed and bound in the UK by Short Run Press

For Tom

Part One

I.

A city scene, viewed from the centre of the street. On either side, six-storey houses, all the same height and yet each with their own character. Some feature elaborate stucco work around the windows. Others have tall entranceways, high enough to accommodate a horse-drawn carriage. There are houses with balconies bolted on to the exterior walls, space for bicycles or boxes of herbs and tomatoes beside small tables and fold-out chairs. At the end of the street the sun hangs low in the sky, casting long shadows. On the pavement a person walks away, a slim silhouette. They wear a long coat that falls down to the back of their knees. No further identifying features.

A hillside of beech trees, their trunks standing tall above a thick layer of leaves on the ground. It is late winter, or early spring. Between the trees black wooden crosses have been hammered into the ground. There is no obvious pattern. A cluster of four, over to the left. A number of pairs. Some stand solitary, leaves bunched at their base. Altogether there are seventeen in view. Seventeen black crosses, although there is a sense that there are more, many more, just out of sight.

A close-up of a gateway of smooth stone, two sides of a corner. To the left, a ghostly sign on the brickwork, the letters faded. It is not possible to read them all, but they suggest that there was once a coal dealer here, a certain P.A. SCH————, with an arrow directing potential customers to the back courtyard. To the right, a brand new brass plaque, all the letters carefully engraved. JOHANNSSEN. ARCHITECTURE + DESIGN BUREAU. Polished: the sign shines in the sun.

A sandy trail through the woods. Tall pines against a bleached sky. The only branches are at the top, far above the forest floor. The path undulates but maintains a straight line between the trees, and at the top of one of the rises stands an oak tree. It is thick, solid. Standing here since long before the pines were planted.

A prison cell, four metres by two. A concrete bed and a barred window, a built-in toilet in the corner. At the centre of the room stands an exhibition display, a soft surface framed by a thin sliver of silver metal, onto which a banner has been pinned. Words of protest, painted on a bed sheet.

A basketball court, empty except for a two-tone ball and discarded soft drink can. Beyond the fence a wide river flows, with a dense forest on the opposite bank, like in a fairy tale. On the river a barge travels against the current, laden with identical cars.

A sand dune out of which tall grass sparsely grows. Beyond, the beach, the sea and the sky. It is impossible to make out the exact place where one meets the other. Wave breakers reach out towards the horizon in straight rows, but today the water is glassy, calm.

A fragmented headstone in three pieces. The visible letters come from the Latin and Hebrew alphabets. Around them, early springtime flowers push their way up through the frosted ground.

A single track railway line. On either side, fir trees lean in over the tracks in the mist, fading in shades to a white centre where nothing can be seen.

Black.

*****

The applause starts quietly, a little hesitant as if we are all waiting for something to happen. Then it rises, like the sound of an approaching train as Pascal's name appears in the centre of the screen. There are about a hundred people in this darkened, windowless room, tucked away in the basement of a London hotel, and they are all applauding my friend. They continue for a while, eyes peering through the darkness to see if they can spot someone who might be him, in case he might be here, listening to their appreciation in this function room with its soft carpets and abstract pastel prints spaced out on the wall. I am concentrating on the moment. Taking it all in, committing as many details as possible to memory, for my friend is not here and I want to be able to tell him as much as I can about what happened when the last of his photographs faded to black and his name appeared on the screen.

Beside the screen a spotlight is turned on, creating a pool of light around a microphone and a slender lectern. A man steps into the light with a piece of paper in his hand. He's wearing jeans and a shirt; his tie is the work of someone who presumably doesn't wear one very often. He looks down at the paper before he begins to speak. The room has stopped clapping now, as we wait to hear what he has to say.

He begins, after a final sip of water, by thanking us all for coming, for taking the time to join him and his colleagues in this celebration of Pascal and his work. He talks about the photographs we have seen and the project they were part of, listing the exhibitions hosted by galleries and museums across Europe, and the publishers of the book, who have also joined us tonight. He explains that it is with sadness he has to announce that Pascal cannot be with us for this moment of tribute. He does not give a reason why, but nevertheless he is sure that Pascal will be delighted to hear how many people braved the miserable weather to come out tonight. The man pauses, perhaps because of stage directions scribbled in his notes, and to his obvious relief there are some in the audience who oblige with gentle laughter. He continues with what is his final line, a parade of clauses building to a climax and the sound of applause once more, and I realise it is my cue, that it is time for me to push back my chair and make my way through the tables towards the light.

II.

Drizzle falls on the Euston Road as I switch my bag from one shoulder to the other, standing in the doorway of a pub to check the time on my phone. Noon. Pascal's award is too big to fit in my bag, so I've had to carry it in my hands. It's a square, glass-like object with a hole through the centre. I'm not sure what it is supposed to represent, but at least it is easy to hold. Water is speckled on the surface from the short walk between the underground station exit and this doorway, and so I wipe it with my sleeve as I look out across the street, through the misting rain and the steady flow of cars, buses and taxis. The sound of a wet road in England is different to where I live now. It must be something to do with the road surfaces, or maybe even the vehicles themselves.

Once I left the country of my childhood I realised those differences were everywhere: in the shape of the street furniture and the painted lines by the side of the road, the strength and colour of the light cast by the streetlamps or the sound of the ambulance sirens as they bounced between the buildings. Of course, every place looks different to another, but I hadn't realised how they sounded different too, and that these two things were connected. We experience a city because of the long story of how it came to be, how it shaped the layout of the streets or the site of the buildings, the present day an end point of a long and individual story. And now, when I return to London or Liverpool, Manchester or Leeds, I find that to rediscover those elements that make a place look and sound as it does is to trigger memories of my own story, many of which I am surprised are still there.

The walk home from football training, legs muddy beneath scratchy school trousers because the changing room showers were broken. The wait for slow drinkers on a university pub crawl, standing on the street between the picnic tables and the bus stop, a night out often attempted but never completed, because halfway through we reached the end of our road and we were drunk enough already. The time here, in London, on a hot summer evening, outside on the steps of a closed laundrette, beers in plastic pint pots, talking with Pascal as it slowly went dark and the streetlamps flickered on above where we sat.

A bus moves through a puddle that has grown above an overwhelmed drain and so I step back, further into the doorway, even though the spray is a long way from reaching me. I use my phone to take a picture and record a snippet of sound. I will send them to Pascal later. He asked me to document the trip. The details were important, he said. The moments of waiting. In all his travels, they were often the experiences that lingered longest.

There is still an hour until my train and the drizzle has turned to rain. The pub door opens and a man pushes past me, stepping out to stand beneath the sodden awning to smoke his cigarette. I feel the warmth of the pub's interior as the door swings, the smell of air freshener and long-spilled beer. Another one of those moments. I step inside.

The pub is quite empty, a cavernous room of patterned carpets and wooden furniture, raised sections and fruit machines by the toilet doors. There are menus on every table and a long line of beer taps behind the bar. It's a place to grab a drink and a bite to eat after work or while waiting for the train, and on this Sunday lunchtime there are only solitary men, sitting with cups of coffee and their phones, and a small group of football fans who came down on the early train, the rain driving them into the first pub they came to outside the station. They are gathered around a stand-up table close to the bar and nurse their beers. Kick-off is still a good few hours away.

I take my pint to a table in the corner by the door, and put it down alongside Pascal's award, my bag tucked away beneath my chair at my feet. Having served me, the barman has come out into the room and is moving from table to table with a collection of wooden boxes, each filled with cutlery and condiments.

'What's this?' the barman says as he reaches me, looking down at the plastic shape next to my pint glass. I tell him about Pascal and his photographs, about how he had asked me to come to London and collect it, and that I was now about to deliver it to him. The barman is having a quiet shift and seems eager to talk. He wants to know where Pascal is now and, when I tell him, I am surprised that he has heard of the island, that he nods in recognition when I say its name. He was there once, the barman says, or at least on the mainland, from where he could see the island low on the horizon from the top of the dunes. It was a church trip, years ago, and they had slept in huge tents a short walk from the beach. Not that he ever went to church any more, he continues, stumbling slightly over his words, his demeanour changing as if he is suddenly aware of what it is he is saying, out loud and to a customer, to a stranger. It was nice there, he says, a little helplessly now. What he remembers most was the view from the top of the dunes, when he would climb up there in the morning and look out across the sea. That, and the fact that there were no tides.

He stops and looks at me, waiting for a response. I tell him about the train, about how I arrived only yesterday at St Pancras and that I am already leaving again, retracing my journey home and then on to the island. The barman has recovered his composure and shakes his head.

'If it was me,' he says, rearranging a couple of sachets of brown sauce in the wooden box on the table between us, 'I'd just fly. Climate change or not.'

I just nod. He gives me a small smile, and then he moves on. I don't tell him that I didn't feel like I had much of a choice, that from the moment Pascal asked me to do this, it was clear I was going to be taking the train. It wasn't that Pascal insisted, or even asked about my travel arrangements, it was just that I knew how he would have come if he could, and so it felt only right for me to do the same. And in any case, he'd given me more than enough to do to fill the time along the way.

As time passes it feels like you can become increasingly close to some people who you never, or hardly ever, get to see. The major beats of life are shared and distributed, liked and commented upon. Subtle changes of appearance, of hair colour and length, of the ageing process, are unconsciously absorbed. Relationships and birthdays, new jobs and a new flat. People might lose touch, but they don't lose track. In the fifteen years between my leaving England and the house I'd shared with Pascal in Leeds, to the evening in London when he came back into my life properly again, I'd seen him in person only twice. Once in Rotterdam, when we both happened to be there for work at the same time. Once in Landeck, in Austria, when we were close enough to meet each other halfway. Those meetings amounted to perhaps five hours together in total. Five hours in fifteen years. And yet thanks to the pictures and posts, the emails and messages, it never felt like we had to play catch up. It never really felt like we'd been apart.

When we met in London, something changed. As we sat by the Kingsland Road and watched the rush hour traffic stream by, I already felt that it would not be another four or five years before we saw each other again. I was in the city for work, for a series of meetings that kept me busy throughout the day but which finished close to a small bookshop near Pascal's flat. It was one of those July days when the heat was such that the road melted beneath the tires of the buses and the air was thick enough to be both energy sapping and yet dense enough to hold a person upright in its warm embrace. We met outside the bookshop and then walked down to the pub on the corner, where all the tables outside were full and the drinkers spilled down the pavement, sitting where they could. I'd bought Pascal a book, a present that I thought he might like, and he accepted it with grace but warned me that he would give it away as soon as he was finished, so I shouldn't write anything inside the cover. I knew what he was like, he said with a shrug, and I did, which was why I hadn't scribbled a message in the book in the first place.

Pascal had always been one to live out of a suitcase. Or a rucksack. Or an old, heavy cardboard box, salvaged from the supermarket. As long as it could be transported on a train or a bus. When we lived together in that house in Leeds, there was nearly nothing there that belonged to Pascal, even though it was his name on the contract and it was to him that the rest of us paid the rent. It was crucial, he said, not to have too much stuff, too many things. You had to be able to carry everything that was important to you. When he left, in his car or on the train, travelling for work as he often did, he took with him everything that was important, as if he might never come back. For the time he was gone, it was like the rest of us in the house were living with a ghost.

I had friends at the time who doubted whether Pascal existed, such was his complete absence in those days and weeks when he was away, photographing a football tournament or a test match, a cycling tour or a rowing regatta. One of our flatmates once asked him, when he explained his philosophy of belongings to her, what it was that he thought was going to happen. What terrible event, she said, was he constantly prepared for? Pascal smiled and simply said that being able to up and leave at any time was not necessarily in anticipation of something bad happening. There were other possibilities too.

That evening in London, sitting on the laundrette steps, we shared a few memories and filled in some gaps, but otherwise we talked little about the past. We didn't need to. As I had realised in Amsterdam and in Austria, time created no distance with Pascal. It simply bent back to let us continue from where we left off.

I first met Pascal in the house on Richmond Mount that we would come to share, having seen an advert for a room in the window of a newsagents on Hyde Park corner. Pascal let me into the house, briefly showed me the living room, the kitchen and the room that would be mine. He asked me a few questions about what I was doing in Leeds while giving me the feeling he wasn't really interested in the answers, and then suggested we went for a walk. We walked from Headingley, past the cricket ground to where the land falls away towards the river, the slopes lined with steep terraces that run down towards the main road, the railway line and the supermarkets and cinemas that occupied the valley floor. Pascal was leading, and we were walking to Kirkstall Abbey, although I didn't know what the destination was going to be until we got there. Once we arrived we wandered the grounds amidst the remains of the Abbey, the sun shining through the gaps in the soot-blackened Yorkshire stone. It had been a ruin, Pascal told me, longer than it had ever been a working abbey, and that was perhaps the key to its longevity. We like ruins better than we like our buildings intact, he said, taking a small camera out of his shoulder bag.

We strolled through the grounds as Pascal took photographs. He asked me questions as we went, about my family and my friends, about girlfriends and what I daydreamed of when sitting in the lecture halls of the university. I answered them all, but asked no questions of my own, mainly because he seemed to be so concentrated on his photographs. He seemed happy to let me talk, to provide the background noise to his work, which he was taking very seriously despite the fact that all he had with him was a very basic, point and shoot camera. He stopped when he reached the end of the roll, and we sat down by the river.

He told me that he thought I was honest; that I wasn't afraid to speak about my relationships and my feelings. It was important in a friendship to be able to do this properly, not hidden behind a bravado that often concealed more than it revealed. As the river rolled by in front of us and the trees cast shadows across the lawn between where we sat and the Abbey behind us, he told me that he was sure he was going to enjoy our conversations. Come on, he said, pulling himself to his feet. He patted me on the shoulder. It was time to celebrate. It was his way of telling me that I'd got the room.

III.

Last night, after the ceremony, I walked back to my hotel with Pascal's award in my hand. I walked because I was scared that if I sat down on a night bus I would fall asleep, drained as I was. I'd left the apartment early in the morning and arrived in London just two hours before the event was due to start, and all the way, through Germany and Belgium, France and under the channel, I'd been listening to Pascal's voice. And as I stepped down from the train under the vaulting roof of St Pancras station to change to the underground, and when I returned to the surface to find a sandwich place to grab a bite to eat before checking into my hotel, he was still there, talking in my ear. The sound of his voice took me away from my immediate surroundings, from the train carriage or the seat at the sandwich shop window to wherever it was he happened to be talking about. It was only later, after I'd left the basement function room, with his award in my hand, that it finally felt like I'd arrived in London. And at that point, there was only another thirteen hours or so before I was due to leave again.

At my hotel I used a four-digit code to get in through the front door and took the lift to the third floor. My room was small, a narrow walkway with a door off to a tiny bathroom, a single bed and a thin desk that was only slightly wider than a sideboard. On it sat a travel kettle and a single mug. One sachet of instant coffee, one thin stick of sugar, and one tea bag. A television had been bolted to the wall in a way that the only way to see it properly would be to perch on the window ledge. None of this mattered to me. It was just a room. A place to sleep.

Still, having put Pascal's award down on the desk, I stepped back in order to take a photograph of this room with my phone. It was part of the process, to document the trip, but it was also a habit that had started since I began working on this project a few months before. I was looking forward to hearing what he thought. He would have opinions on this room that he would want to share, and I knew he would like to see it. Hotel rooms are his kind of place.

I lifted my bag up onto the bed. Unzipping it, I pulled out a cardboard folder that was resting on top of my change of clothes. The folder was full of photographs, printed in A5. I took them out and began to flick through. I was searching for hotel rooms, for places that reminded me of the one that I now found myself in.

I don't know why. I was dead tired and moving on autopilot. Maybe it was so I could refer to it in any message I sent with my own photograph to Pascal; to offer up a hint of a place it might have reminded him of, a place from his own collection of photographs and memories. Another hotel room in another land could substitute for this corner room in a scruffy London hotel. The last room in the corridor, next to the lift, where the streetlight shone in through the blackout curtain I hadn't properly closed, and where I would fall asleep to the sound of taxis drifting through the puddles that had gathered by the side of the road beneath the window. Perhaps he would see my photograph, and be taken away from the island for a moment, to another city, where the taxis drifting through the puddles sounded similar, but not the same, as the ones I could hear in London.

In the pub on the Euston Road, waiting for the train, I sip my pint and for the first time today, pull the headphones out from my pocket. The sound of the pub retreats as Pascal's familiar voice fills my ears.

'There is a part of me, Ben,' Pascal says, 'that wishes I was born at a different time. Do you have this feeling too? I don't think this is an unfamiliar wish. I think many of us think this at some point or other in our lives. We'd like to have been there on the barricades in 1968. Or at Woodstock. Or the very first Glastonbury. We'd like to have seen Pele playing in his prime or roamed the streets of Berlin with Christopher Isherwood. For me, I always wish I had lived at a time when it was possible, for some people in this world at least, to live out their days in hotel rooms.

I'm not talking about some kind of skid row flophouse where the reception desk is behind bulletproof glass and the dossers and drifters are collapsed into old sofas in the lobby. I mean respectable hotels, where you could live and be looked after, and spend your time worrying about your work or your love life, and not about laundry or cooking or paying the electricity bill. There was a time, when I was younger, maybe at university but in any event just before we met, when I thought it still might be possible. There were places where people still did it. You've heard about the famous one in New York? Everyone knows about that one. But I was sure there must be others too. In Mexico City or Bangkok. In Prague, because it was still cheap back then. Or in Budapest, where it was cheaper still.

I had this notion, based on reading too many books, wanting to live in the world of those books rather than the one we had, and it was a foolish notion I think, but what I wanted was to be with all the freaks and weirdos, to be part of that community who have opted out of normal society and are making their way through life on their talent and genius. You remember those stories we wrote? Sitting up in my room with a typewriter and a bottle of Jack Daniels. Oh God, I'm embarrassed to think about it even now. Embarrassed but maybe also a little curious to read them again. This is part of who we are and who I was, so it needs to be said. It needs to be included. I had this vision, around the time we first met, that it was going to be just me, my bag and my camera. It was all I would need to make my way, like a busker's guitar.

When I'm not feeling too hard on my younger self, I recognise that part of me knew I was a fool even then. Just another of those earnest young literary men who have read too much Kerouac and Hesse, and not enough women. We thought we'd found a shortcut to authenticity. To an authentic life, whatever the hell that means. By the time we met I was already over the worst of it. There was the occasional relapse, with the typewriter and the bourbon, but if I remember rightly you did most of the writing anyway. I liked the words better when they were still in my head.

No, by then I'd worked out that my camera could be my busker's guitar, but there was easier money to be made using it to record the achievements of others rather than for any great artistic vision of my own. I could capture the joy of victory, the anguish of defeat. The desperate dive for the line and the majestic swing of a bat. It could all be captured through my telephoto lens.

But as I went through this process, working out how to make it work for me, I never lost my love of hotel rooms. It never diminished over the years, even after thousands of assignments. The press trips and expeditions. If anything, the appeal grew stronger. Can you understand that? Most people can't. They profess to like hotel rooms, especially ones which are *nice* or which are *fancy*. Somewhere to stay that gives them something to show off about when they get home. But I think most people are happy to leave eventually, however nice the hotel might be, however luxurious and privileged it makes them feel. They are happy to go home. I know it because they told me. My fellow photographers. The journalists and the producers. Other guests, who I met over a late drink at the bar. After a while they were all ready to leave. But not me. I didn't feel it.'

I finish my drink and hoist my bag onto my shoulder. I step out into the rain, pulling my hood up over my head, tucking Pascal's award under my jacket, even though it is made of plastic. As I hurry down the street to the station, Pascal continues to talk.

*****

'I think it is clearer to me now than it was back then,' Pascal says. 'Perhaps it is because I cannot see when I will stay in a hotel again. They have always spoken to me, and they speak to me still from a great distance. I think it's the simple fact that from the moment they open their doors and welcome their very first guests, they are already in the process of becoming out of date. Out of time. It is impossible, unless a hotel is to renovate and redecorate on an almost permanent basis, to keep up with the times, with the dictates of fashion. In that sense, a hotel is a lot like a map. From the moment they are put out into the world, they are already out of time. Old-fashioned. Last season's colours. Furniture from another decade. Prints on the wall from another century.

This is what I like. Especially this. The sense of being out of time. Or that time has *stopped*. You don't really exist any more in your normal, everyday world. None of your routines matter. I always thought, checking into another hotel room, into another anonymous place where the normal strictures of my life no longer applied, that if time has stopped, well, in this place at least, that must make me immortal.

Can you hear that I am smiling, Ben? Should I resurrect my dream? Once I wondered if it was a viable plan for my retirement. That I could live out my days in a series of modest hotel rooms. It's probably the only long-term plan I ever had. Please make sure this is in there. Desires unrealised are just as important as those that were fulfilled. Especially now.'

*****

The recording ends as I enter St Pancras station, heading to the Eurostar terminal entrance, below the platforms among the shops. A young woman sits at a piano with a supermarket bag at her feet and plays a tune, recognisable but unnameable to most who stop and listen. I am the same. It is one of those pieces of music that is often used in adverts or in a film score, the soundtrack to the final montage of a live television event. I have presumably heard it played by some of the world's finest musicians and by buskers in the shopping precinct. And now by this young woman taking a break from her shopping.

She plays it well, with joy on her face as her fingers dance across the keyboard. When she finishes there is a smattering of polite applause as she vacates the stool, picks up her shopping bag, and melts into the crowd. The rest of us wait for a moment, to see if anyone will step forward to take her place. But no one does, and we begin to drift off, each returning to what had preoccupied us before she started to play.

I move quickly through the ticket check and passport controls, the security scan and the other elements that make this like no other train journey I've ever made. But however close this might feel to flying, there is a platform at the end of the rigmarole, and for the purpose of this trip, it had to be the train. At the cafe I pick up a coffee and then find a seat, pulling out my notepad and my phone, searching through the files, until I find the one that I'm looking for. It is linked to a photograph in my bag. An overnight train, somewhere in Asia.

*****

'To my mind,' Pascal says, 'the train is the crowning achievement of human transportation. It is a collective solution to a particular problem, a means of getting us from A to B that is social, that brings people together. Why do you think we have novels set on trains, or films? People can meet in their compartment or the dining car. They can fall in love. Make friends. Smoke cigarettes together or plot the downfall of a government. They can decide, on a whim, to cut short their journey at the next station or extend it to the very end of the line in order to carry on a conversation they've already begun. We created this brilliant thing, this perfect thing, and then we nearly destroyed it. We spurned it for the car, for the individual freedom of the automobile. To my mind the train is a symbol of the best of what we can do. The car is symbolic of everything that has gone wrong in our society.'

*****

I wait out the pause, my pen poised. I can hear Pascal sigh.

*****

'Don't mind me,' Pascal says. 'I'm just not... There's basically no cars on the island. Isn't that great? No trains either, but still. Anyway, it's about solidarity, I think. Solidarity, yes. That's the best way to put it. It's about solidarity, and that's why we should take the train.'

*****

Beneath the huge, arching roof of St Pancras I walk along the platform until I find my carriage and climb aboard. Settling in to my seat, I pull out the folder of photographs and put it with my notepad on the little table in front of me. I'm one of the first onto the train, but as I settle into my work it fills up around me. A woman sits down next to me, with a German book in her hand and a set of headphones of her own. She makes no acknowledgement of my presence or our closeness. There does not seem to be much of Pascal's sense of solidarity on offer, not on this particular train, not today.

IV.

There were a couple of times, back in Leeds, when Pascal and I walked or took the bus down into town and caught the Ilkley train to the end of the line. It wasn't a long journey, through Guiseley and into Wharfedale, and we could have driven in the battered old Mini that Pascal used for work, but even back then he preferred to take the train. From the station at Ilkley we would walk to the end of the platform and into town, following the streets that led from the centre down in the valley up the sides of the hills that led onto the moor. The roads were steep, and at the top, where the last of the houses gave way to open countryside, we tiptoed over cattle grids as we left the protection of the town and felt the wind on our faces for the first time.

We had a route that we followed, although if you took me there now I wouldn't be able to show you. It was Pascal's route, Pascal's tradition, and I wasn't the first of the flatmates to be taken up there to the heather and the millstone grit outcrops. The first time we went, we were both nursing hangovers from a long night in the pub. It was March and the weather was foul. The wind and rain whipped across the tops of the moor, our jackets flapping like untethered tent doors. I was miserable, feeling the water seep in through the seams of my waterproof and the tops of my trainers, while Pascal walked with grim determination until he reached his chosen spot.

Despite the low cloud and rain there was still a view, of the rolling contours of the land, of how the glaciers and the rivers had shaped everything we were looking at, where the moors were wild and free and the towns and villages were huddled down in the cracks of the land, as if in search of protection. Pascal tried to tell me something but the wind was too loud, and so we stood side by side for a while until he had seen enough, and then we followed a path that seemed to have no real direction in mind until it led us to the Cow and Calf rocks and the warmth of the pub a little way down the road.

He came to the moors for the view, he told me, as we nursed pints that our stomachs were still not really ready for. When he had chosen Leeds, he said, he hadn't really thought about how far away it was from the sea. About how much he would miss the view, the sense of endlessness that you get when you stand a little way up from the shore and look out towards the horizon. Up on the rocks, he said, he had something of that feeling, even on a grey day like today. And when the weather was fine, he could imagine that if he looked closely enough, he could see the waves breaking on the surface of the North Sea.

We sat a little longer in the pub until our beers were finished and then walked back into Ilkley, picking up sausage rolls from a bakery by the station to eat on the train. We made that trip at least six or seven times in the period we lived together, and it always felt like something of an escape. With each station out along the train line we left our normal life behind, and with each station on the return we were brought back, so that by the time we stepped down from the train at Leeds and walked down the platform towards the barriers, it felt a little bit like we hadn't been anywhere at all, and the heather and the wind, the rocks and the grass, were all as much a product of the imagination as Pascal's waves crashing down on the horizon.

I remember another station and another vaulting roof. Six months ago I travelled to Hamburg to meet Pascal at a tiny bar at the end of the station, overlooking the platforms. Hamburg station always felt cluttered to me, a confusing space where the ceilings of the shops are too low, the walkways narrow and confining, and it is filled with too many people. Even on the brightest days outside, the light seems to struggle through the dirty glass of the roof, creating the atmosphere of an old movie set, a space of dust-filled light columns and gloomy, shadowy corners, that hints at the memory of the steam engine smoke that once gathered there.

It was no different when I met Pascal, sitting at the bar above the platforms with a narrow glass of pilsner in front of him and his bags at his feet. He had messaged me only a few days before to say that his plans had changed, and that he would no longer be able to come to us. But could I come to meet him? Since that night in London he had been to Germany many times and I'd seen him often, as he travelled back and forth from his flat on the Eurostar, criss-crossing the country, to take the photographs that would win him the award. By the time we met in Hamburg he was done. The exhibitions in London, Düsseldorf and Basel had been a success. The book was about to be published.

Could I come to Hamburg? he'd asked via text message. He didn't have much time, but there was a gap between his trains if I could make it. It was a long round trip for a beer, but I agreed.

He was talking to the barman as I approached, and as always it was something of a shock to hear him speaking in his mother tongue. Back in Leeds, I don't think I ever heard him speaking anything other than English, with his soft, Scouse-inflected accent. Now he was speaking German with the barman, discussing trains and how Deutsche Bahn was losing its reputation for punctuality. After all, he said, turning to face me but still talking to the barman, his friend was twenty minutes late, and that was because the Berlin train was always twenty minutes late. He stood up off the stool and gave me a hug.

We sat down and he ordered me a drink and then, without any further small-talk or chat, he told me his news. At least, he told me what he considered was enough for me to know. He was sick, he said, his eyes locked on mine. He was very sick. It made him tired, and it was only going to get worse. He told me that I shouldn't worry, that he wasn't going anywhere anytime soon, but that the illness had given him lots to think about. He was struggling, mentally and physically, and he realised that whatever happened in the future, the time available, like his energy, was finite. So it was time, he continued, to do something about a project he had been working on for years, one that he had started the very day he got his first camera and had continued ever since. Now was the time to pull it all together, Pascal said, turning away from me now. But he needed my help.

It was a lot to take in. I sat there for a moment, still looking at him, as he gazed absently at the bottles of spirits on the back of the bar. I tried to find the right words but I couldn't reach them.

He was often too tired to write, he said, continuing through my silence. He had already found the Germany book hard, and he didn't think he could manage another. The computer screen made his eyes ache and his hands hadn't held a pen, not properly, in years. Who had? It was not the time to start again. So he needed a writer.

I think here I was able to get some words out, a mumbled sentence that he didn't let me finish. He reminded me I had always been better with words. That it would come back to me. What he wanted was clear. He would send me the photographs and he would record what he wanted to say about them. Speaking, he said ruefully, hadn't yet become a problem. So he would speak, and record, and get it all out and get it all down, and I would try and bring some order to it. Could I do that?

A ghostwriter, I said. That's what he wanted me to be.

Pascal looked up at me again and narrowed his eyes, took a mouthful of beer and then wiped the foam from his top lip with the back of his hand.

He wasn't planning on being a ghost just yet, he said, and then lifted up his glass. We drank a toast, and with the clink of the glasses it was agreed. Pascal suggested another round. There was still half an hour until my train back to Berlin, and from where we were sitting it was possible to read on the platform displays below that it was running late.

Outside the train window, Kent passes by in the rain. Fields and small patches of woodland. Quiet towns of low-slung buildings huddled around a church spire. A sense that the city and sea are close, just over the horizon. I've laid out four photographs on the small table in front of me as my neighbour continues to read her book. Page after page of unbroken text, by a writer who doesn't seem to believe in paragraphs.

Number one. A large room with a bay window at one end, beneath which a sofa bed has been unfolded. The bedding is slept in and rumpled, and in place of curtains there are blankets hanging in the window, lopsided to allow a flare of morning sunshine in through the glass in the corner. In front of the sofa bed is a coffee table, on which there is an ashtray, three books, two opened and placed face down, and a candle. The wax has spilled down the sides and over the rim of the small plate that was supposed to contain it, onto the wooden table top.

Number two. A cabin on a ferry. A bunk bed with two bunks and a small table in the corner. No porthole and no view of the outside. The bedding is folded neatly at the end of each bunk, with a miserly pillow at the other. Everything on view seems to be bleached somehow, an off-white, milky filter, that makes the red and greens of the emergency exit plan all the more striking, hanging as it is on the wall beside a tiny mirror.

Number three. A room I recognise. It is Pascal's bedroom in Leeds, on the ground floor by the front door. When you came into the house, the living room and kitchen were on one side of the hall and Pascal's room was on the other. The rest of us slept upstairs. When he was away on a job we were allowed to use his room, the door left propped open for this purpose. There was a television in the corner and an armchair in the window. Our friends could sleep over in his bed if they wanted, as long as we remembered to change the sheets before he came home.

Number four. A hotel room. There are many, many hotel rooms. I haven't counted them all. In the front of my notebook I have tried to create an index, to help me identify which photo is from where. I look down my list to match the number with the one written in pencil and circled on the back of the photograph.

Hotel room in Croatia. Possibly Makarska. Maybe Trogir. Summer 1988.

Pascal would have been fifteen. He would have had the camera for just over a year. He would have been on holiday with his parents. His mother was still alive. I haven't listened to all the recordings yet. I don't know if he has spoken about this room, or this trip. We knew from the beginning we wouldn't be able to use them all. In the three decades since he was given the camera, Pascal has slept in a lot of rooms. They all have a story, I'm sure. But not all stories need to be told.

*****

'We took the ferry to Norway,' Pascal says. 'From Newcastle to Stavanger. I was about seventeen. My father always wanted to see the fjords. He had a postcard on his study wall that a friend sent him in the late 1980s. It had always been the plan, but they just never got round to it. That summer he decided we would go, the two of us. We packed the car and drove up from Merseyside. I don't remember much about the ferry apart from the buffet, and the fact that the crossing was a bit rocky. Dad was quiet. He spent a lot of time on deck, looking at the sea. He was watching the white horses.

We were both very quiet then. I think he planned the trip because he knew it meant we would have to spend a lot of time together. We would be sharing rooms, sharing a tent. There would be lots to look at and things to talk about. Other things. And there would be time enough for silence and time enough to speak.

We stayed in many places on that trip but apart from the ferry I only took one other photograph. It was the inside of the tent, which of course remained the same wherever we pitched it, whether we were in the shadow of a mountain or overlooking the sea, and I didn't want to waste the film. Altogether we spent two months in Norway. I was in the middle of my A Levels, the summer break from college. Dad was still on compassionate leave. We had so much time. Enough time.

I wonder if I should ask him now if he remembers that trip. Whether he remembers the conversations, the silence. Whether he remembers the one campsite where it never seemed to stop raining and the Dutch guy let me ride his motorbike up and down the lane. He told my Dad not to worry, that the sidecar would make it impossible to fall off as long as I didn't attempt any sharp turns.

I remember riding back through the entrance of the campsite. The rain was easing off and there was mist rising up off the grass. It was so green. I can still see it if I close my eyes. How green it was. My dad was standing next to the Dutch guy. All I could hear was the motorbike engine, and all I could smell was oil and petrol and exhaust. The Dutch guy was smiling, patting my dad on his back. And my dad was smiling too, because after all the Dutch guy couldn't possibly know what he was feeling inside, and we were just three men on a campsite with time to kill as we waited for the rain to stop and a motorbike with an engine that echoed through the valley and that you couldn't fall off.

That night was the first time I got drunk with my dad. Red wine from a box we'd brought from home. We shared it with the Dutch guy. We never did find out why he was riding with a sidecar when he was travelling alone.'

V.

When I think back on that time with Pascal in Leeds, sharing the house on Richmond Mount, the three years we lived together feel foggy and blurred, the timeline skewed, with fragmentary moments of clarity, vivid memories returned and then lost again. With the other flatmates, all of us studying, we fell into routines that made one week feel much like the next. The walk down the hill into university. Drinking in one of three or four favourite pubs. Long afternoons blending into evenings in the living room, watching television from sunken sofas and armchairs that the landlord had installed more than a decade before.

Pascal was away working most weekends and often in the evening. He remained a little distant from the rest of us. But if he generally kept us at arm's length, he was also capable of much kindness and loyalty. Early on in my time in the house, my dad had an accident and was rushed to hospital. It was Pascal who took the call, as I was out at the shops, or on my way home from university. I don't remember now. What I do remember is that he was waiting for me in the doorway of his bedroom as I opened the front door. He already had his jacket on, the keys to his Mini hanging from a finger. I wasn't to worry, he said, but we had to leave. He told me what my mum had said, that it was going to be okay but that my dad would have to have an operation. Pascal had already told her he would drive me, that we would be there in a couple of hours.

We crossed the Pennines on the M62 in black and white. That's how I remember it now, like an old film spooling across the windscreen as we drove. Grey skies and dark moors. Monochrome lorries and whitewashed farmhouses. The Mini was low to the road and it felt like we could get sucked under wheels that seemed to be towering over our heads, but I wasn't scared. Not of that, not of the road, but what was at the end of it.

At the hospital we met my mum in the waiting room. He was in the operating theatre and would be there for a number of hours. The doctors had told her to go home but she'd been waiting for us. None of us had a mobile phone then, and we'd arranged to meet at the hospital, so that was where she'd stayed. Pascal drove us back to the house, down the back lanes rather than the main road, as if approaching our village by stealth. In the kitchen we sat around the table and sipped our tea, eyes on the clock above the cooker until it was time to return to the hospital. It felt strange to have Pascal there, two realities colliding unexpectedly. He looked over my childhood photographs and those of my sister, making fun of our jumpers and cords, socks and sandals on a Scottish camping holiday. When he went to the toilet my mum told me he seemed like a good friend, and I told her that he was, although when she asked me about his background I realised how little I knew.

My dad made a full recovery. Pascal left me at home as he had to return to Leeds to cover a Champion's League match at Elland Road, and a few days later, with my dad recuperating at home, I followed him back across the Pennines. The first thing he told me when we met in the kitchen at Richmond Mount was that he liked our house. It felt like a home, he said. It reminded him of where he'd grown up. And then he took his cup of tea through the living room to his bedroom, and gently shut the door.

Beyond the train window is only darkness. We're crossing the channel, passing beneath. I remember the television news the day the two sides of the tunnel met, my mum calling me in from the garden to watch. Hands reaching through a small hole. Men in hard hats and little plastic flags. An island no more. Tethered. And not even fog in the channel could cut us off.

What did I know about Pascal back when we lived together? I knew that he was born in Germany, that he had moved to England as a child and that he grew up near Southport, just a few miles from where my parents lived. I knew that his father was a lecturer and his mother had died suddenly, of a heart attack when Pascal was sixteen. These were the biographical basics, the kind of information you learned about university friends during a first evening in the pub together. But with Pascal, it never went deeper than that, even though he was more than interested in us, always asking questions, but never offering up information about himself. In conversation he was open and straightforward, he never felt evasive, and yet he left very little of himself behind. There were hints at things, moments when he left himself a bit more exposed than he would have probably liked, but if you were not concentrating then you might just miss it.

There was one story he did like to tell, one that I must have heard three or four times during the years in Leeds, usually when someone new moved into one of the rooms upstairs or someone brought a new face around to hang out in the living room. He was born in the GDR, he would say, in East Germany. Born on 7 October 1972, when the GDR was celebrating its own birthday. It was a story of their family, he said, part of the mythology. All families have their founding stories, like nations, he said. It involved his mother in hospital, giving birth, while his father found himself stuck on the other side of the birthday parade, unable to get across the river of people and their flags, his way blocked. His father would try to help him picture the scene, stuck at the barricades, about to miss the birth of his son because of the parade. Because of the spectacle. His mum said that she had never been as angry at his father as she was in that moment, but that later, especially after they'd gone, she liked the story because its absurdity seemed fitting for the place they'd left behind.

That was the only real story Pascal told, a memory from his childhood that he couldn't possibly remember. In a family, the stories that are passed down are the ones we want to be told, Pascal said, and it seemed back then that there were no others that he wished to share, except for a brief tale about his fourteenth birthday and being given his first camera. It was the moment when he realised that it was what he wanted to do with his life. 7 October 1986. The German Democratic Republic was 37 years old, as Pascal tested his new toy by photographing his bedroom from the doorway. Four years later, Pascal was still taking photographs. The GDR no longer existed.

*****

A small room, simply furnished. A single bed against one wall. A desk against the wall opposite. A chest of drawers stands beneath the window, which takes up half of the back wall of the room. The other half is filled with a poster of Kenny Dalglish, arms aloft. The bed is made, with a light blue duvet cover. On the top of the chest of drawers are some constructions made of Lego, while against the back of the desk is a row of books. The room is clean and tidy, ready to be presented to the world. Or for a birthday party. Whether or not it was the photographer himself who tidied it is undocumented.

'From my bedroom window,' Pascal says, 'I could see across the street to the houses on the opposite side and, through a gap between two sets of semi-detached, I could also see the dunes. It was for this reason that my mum chose the house. She wanted to be close to the beach, close to the dunes. It reminded her of home, of where she grew up. She would say that just because she was happy to be here, didn't mean she wasn't often thinking of there.

We'd go for walks most weekends, through the dunes to where the pine forests met the beach. There were squirrels there, red ones. The last survivors. We would do these walks whatever the weather, and at all times of the year. Sometimes I would moan, complain about the rain and wind and the fact that we were the only ones stupid enough to be out and about in it, the only ones not sitting inside watching television or listening to the football scores come in on the radio. She would just say that it wasn't really that cold, and then she would tell me stories about the winters when the Baltic froze, the waves that had been about to hit the shore curled and stopped in time, the ice covering the inland sea so thick that the army could drive their tanks across it and the island was an island no more.

So what was a little wind and rain compared to that? And anyway, I remember her saying, a walk by the sea only made sense if the wind was strong enough to blow all your cares away. Otherwise what was the point?

After she died it was a long time before my father and I made that walk. Instead, we would get in the car and he would drive us to places we'd never been before. Places like the Forest of Bowland or the moors around Rivington Pike and Winter Hill, places that were empty of memories. To walk through the dunes at the end of our road and onto the beach would be just too painful. It was our unspoken agreement. And when we finally did, it was as hard as we'd imagined.

She was there with us, every step of the way. Her memory and her absence. It was in that time I began to understand how she'd been the link between us all, the one who held us together and gave form to our family and our relationships. The gap she left was not only what she'd been to us as individuals, as my mother and my father's partner, but also in the space between us two men. She was the interpreter, the one who had always been able to bridge that gap. When she was gone, it was as if my father and I had to almost begin again, as if we were strangers. We had to start from scratch. When we walked through the forest or up on the moors, we rarely fell in step. One would always be leading, half a stride ahead of the other.'

*****

On the train my neighbour is sleeping, her slow and steady breathing dropping every so often into a gentle snore. We are moving quickly now, racing through the countryside with a mid-afternoon sun still high in the sky. I bring the photographs together in a neat pile, to make space for my notebook, Pascal's bedroom on top, Kenny Dalglish forever celebrating his goal.

*****

'The room next door to my bedroom was my father's study,' Pascal says. 'When I sat at the window and looked out across the street, through the houses to the dunes, he would be sitting almost beside me, at his desk on the other side of the wall. The view through his window was close to mine but of course not identical, and the angle wasn't quite right to allow him to see through the houses to the dunes beyond. In those first few months after my mother died we spent a lot of time in those rooms, close but divided. We'd meet downstairs in the kitchen, sharing information about school and work, about what was happening to us beyond the walls of our house, but very little about what was happening within. We tried to negotiate her absence while grieving. It took time.

From where I am sitting now I can also see dunes, rising up beyond the fence at the bottom of the garden. My father is outside, on the terrace just below my window. When the weather is fine he spends a lot of time out there, with his books or just looking out towards the sea. She would be glad to know that we're here together, I think. That we made it back. Despite everything, she would be glad.'

*****

I look out of the window and try to work out where we are, whether we're still in France or if we've already crossed the border into Belgium. I search for clues in the back gardens and farmyards that pass by beneath us. I try to read the number plates of the cars waiting patiently at level crossings for us to pass. We're moving at speed but still I can spy the kids on trampolines and the soft haze above lit barbecues, a gardener bent double over a raised bed and a figure at the kitchen window, taking a break from the dishes to watch us go by.

The houses on the edge of a town give way to scrap yards, bottling plants and superstores, huge expanses of tarmac filled with rows of parked cars or stacks of shipping containers. A waterworks and an industrial estate, a motorway coming over to meet the railway tracks, running alongside us for a while. I catch a glimpse of bilingual road signs and can see for sure that we are in Belgium now, the destinations that lie beyond otherwise invisible borders marked out with circled letters, a code that reads NL, L, D. The motorway pulls away again, striking out on its own, replaced in my view by flat fields, drainage ditches running away in straight lines between them as a solitary bird of prey hovers in the sky above. I turn back to the photographs.

VI.

A rectangular room, all black lines and right angles. A floor of tatami mats and a single mattress at its centre, the covers rumpled after a night's sleep, breaking the order of the room. On the floor beside the bed is a book, open and face down, and by the foot of the bed a pile of dark clothes. It is possible to make out a pair of socks and a t-shirt. The translucent doors at the back of the room have been half opened to reveal a small balcony with two chairs, a table and an ashtray. Beyond the balcony is a wall of greenery, broad-leaved trees or bushes, packed together. From the light and the colour of the leaves it looks like it was recently raining, but that the rain has now stopped.

'It was a football tournament in Japan,' Pascal says, 'a year before the World Cup. Do you remember? I was hired to join the Canada squad, to follow them through the training camp and then the games. I took photos of their training sessions and in the hotels, of the transport to the stadium and even in the dressing room. I wasn't allowed to photograph the matches as they played, but there was always a ticket for me so that I could watch in the stands. It was a fun job.

Once they were knocked out of the tournament the team immediately disbanded, catching flights to wherever in the world they actually lived. Not many of them were based in Canada. After they were gone my time was my own, and I took a train to Tokyo and from there out into the hills. It was a small place, and I can't remember who told me about it. A

35

depressing looking town on this tiny branch line. The train only had one carriage, and although it was pretty full when we got on board, as the hours passed and the train moved from station to station it emptied out, until it was only me and the writer I was travelling with. She had worked in Japan for years, and spoke some of the language, which was good as otherwise I don't think I could have made it on my own.

They picked us up in an old minibus at the station. By the platform there were wooden signs, hiking maps engraved in the surface, leading off into the forest. By the station the houses were neither old nor new, but they all looked cheaply built, and it surprised me. Like the minibus. I had this idea, this impression, that Japan was a place where everything was either traditional or hyper-modern, with nothing in between. But the little train and the town, and especially the minibus, had all seen better days. Our driver had to really rev the engine, making it scream, just to get up the inclines as we followed a road by a winding river. The seats sagged and the seatbelts didn't work. Outside, everything was distorted by the mist that mingled with low clouds. Above us, only grey. Down at the bottom of the gorge, the river raced by, as if in a hurry to reach the sea.

The hotel was a hot spring spa. A Ryokan, with the mat floors and the futon mattresses, but what the photo doesn't show is that it was like any other hotel built in the 1970s or 1980s. The hallways were long and echoey, the paint on the walls faded and the carpets heavy duty and yet so old they'd become threadbare. There were timer lights and glowing fire escape signs. The smell of disinfectant. In the lobby there was a line-up of machines selling snacks and drinks, the surface of the reception desk some kind of fake marble. To step into my bedroom, what you see in the photograph, was to take part in an illusion.

I still have some other pictures from that trip. The light outside the stadiums, in the early evening as the sun went down, was like nothing I'd ever experienced before. I collected all kinds of magazines and newspapers, even though I couldn't read a word. I wanted a record of the games I'd seen. It wasn't like me, this collecting. Perhaps it was because I couldn't read anything, I don't know. Back home I framed a spread from a match report of one of Japan's games. I can still see the photographs, conjure them up in my mind, although I have no idea where that picture frame is. Kawaguchi in goal, lining up the wall when defending a free kick. A crowd scene, all the faces turned in the same direction, thousands of people following the action while the photographer looks the other way. A close up of Ono after he's scored a goal, shaved head and sad eyes. A massive smile on his face.

That trip was supposed to be a preparation for the next year. I was testing my relationship with the writer, to see if we could work together during the World Cup. She'd already lined up some contracts, and we got on well together. It wasn't her fault. But in Japan I started to realise that I didn't want to do sports photography any more. Perhaps it was because I wasn't allowed to shoot the games, that for the first time in years I was free to simply watch the action unfold. I realised how much I had missed and how my work was destroying my love for something that had been so important in my life.

A great game had become defined not by what happened on the pitch, the events that unfolded and the stories they contained, but what I came out with at the final whistle. What images I had, in my film or on my memory card. The photographs I could sell. And I was questioning even the point. Surely the task I had set myself was simply impossible? I was taking something fluid, something with a structure, a narrative, a story, and I was trying to fix it in time. I was trying to capture its essence in one image. How is that possible?

The thing is, I know that it is possible. I have seen it done. Of course it can be. Just perhaps not by me.'

*****

37

On the outskirts of Brussels the nondescript buildings of the suburbs pass by outside the window. High-rise housing estates and more modern, gated apartment complexes. Warehouses containing wholesalers of flowers and vegetables, alcoholic drinks and garden supplies. Motorways and waterways. Railways and criss-crossing pipelines and wires strung between enormous pylons. My neighbour still sleeps, her book fallen forward from her knees, trapped against the seat in front.

*****

'A few years ago I was in a steakhouse in Amsterdam,' Pascal says. 'It was on a small residential street, about fifteen minutes' walk from the main station. It was Argentinian, and in the toilet, above the single urinal, was a photograph of Diego Maradona. You probably know the one. It's one of the most famous. Maradona is closest to the camera, the ball at his instep, his curly hair down over his collar, above the black number 10 on his blue and white shirt. In front, facing Maradona and the ball are six Belgian players. Over half the team. Two are moving to the right. One has made a step to the left. The three in the middle seem to be standing dead still, mesmerised. They are all waiting. Waiting to see what Maradona does next.

That photograph is something of an illusion, an entirely unlikely image made possible by a set of fleeting circumstances that never came together at any other moment during that football match. And yet it somehow tells the story not only of a game between Argentina and Belgium, but in a way, it is the story of the whole of that World Cup and perhaps even Maradona's career. Maybe even the story of the man himself. Diego against the world. And at one point in time, in Mexico in 1986, he was going to do it, and he was going to win.

I have seen that photograph so many times, and yet in Amsterdam I stood in that toilet and stared at it for ages. The way Maradona holds his body. Only he knows what is going to happen next. The Belgian players, their tension and fear and anticipation all readable in their bodies. The green of the pitch. The colours of the shirts. All captured in the open and close of a shutter. A man. His story. His genius.

Later, I looked up stories about the photograph. I saw film footage that explains how such an unlikely scene came to be, and that it is not quite what it seems. But it doesn't matter, because even if it is something of an illusion, it tells a greater truth. I looked up the photographer's name. Steve Powell, working for Sports Illustrated. I'd love to buy him a beer.

Maybe he got lucky. Maybe if I'd kept going, if I'd gone back to Japan and Korea, I would have got lucky also. There might have been one of my photographs discussed in newspaper articles decades later, talked about on photography courses and hanging above the urinals of patriotic restaurants a long way from home. I rarely look at the photographs I took back then, but when I do, I realise that I have no memory of anything else that took place on those pitches or running tracks, in those stadiums. I was trying to show people what they had missed, help them understand what had taken place, but my own understanding was as limited as what I could see through the viewfinder.

In Japan I realised I needed to find a different way. I needed to find a subject that I could have more control over. It is the drama of sport, it's the unwritable quality, that makes us love it. The unpredictability of football is what allowed me to fall in love with it again, once it was no longer part of my job to help tell the story. In Japan I knew that if I was to fall in love again, if it was to mean something to me again, then I would have to let it go. I would have to leave it alone. I would have to go in search of something else. Of other stories.'

*****

If that is how Pascal felt at the time, when he came home from Japan to our house that we still shared in Leeds, I don't remember him telling me. And before the trip I always felt he was more than happy with his job. Proud, even. We would sit in

39

our living room, on those saggy sofas, as a game played out on the television and Pascal explained it to me. Sports photography was storytelling at its finest, he would say, it was the conflict encapsulated. The moment of triumph, the moment of defeat. I have no memory of him voicing any doubts.

We arrive in Brussels, where late afternoon sun casts long shadows across the concrete plaza outside the station exit. The grey skies and drizzle of London feel like a long way away now. I sit down on a plastic chair outside a bistro on the ground floor of an office block. At the table next to me two men talk about what happened in their meeting at work that day. They drink half-litre beers and speak English with unplaceable accents honed at a certain type of school. Their chat is light-hearted, as they wait for their train to whisk them back beneath the channel and home, but there is an underlying current of competition in their words as they discuss the reactions to different parts of their presentation.

I order a beer of my own and something to eat, and as I wait for my food to arrive the plaza fills with soldiers in fatigues, spreading out across the square in front of the station entrance with their guns at the ready. As they move, the few pedestrians caught in the open space hurry along. It's like a scene from the news and yet if I walked twenty paces forward I would be in the middle of it. Armoured vehicles stand at either end of the plaza, as if setting up for a siege. What I notice is that it is all strangely quiet, except for the sound of a helicopter, hovering high above us against the deepening blue sky.

There is a presence at my shoulder and I look up to see the waiter, watching the scene as it unfolds. He tells me not to worry, that I shouldn't be alarmed. It is just a security operation, he says. A test. If there was anything we should be concerned about then we would know about it by now. His colleague arrives with my beer and they say something to each other in French, words that I do not understand, but there is no concern in their tone. The English men are quietened now, as we sit in our front row seats and watch the soldiers fan out further and the armoured cars move slowly across the plaza until they are blocking the station doors.

Terrorism or training, one of the English men says. It is getting to be every week, the other one replies. He looks at his watch. He's wondering if whatever is happening will be over in time for him to catch his train. I sip my beer and sit back. I have time. My train to Aachen is not for an hour or so yet. Aachen, and the last invisible border of my trip; crossing back to Germany.

VII.

It was as Pascal returned from Japan that I made my own plans to leave. University was finished, and I had no concept of what I was supposed to do next and so I decided to travel. As Pascal unpacked, stuffing clothes into the washing machine in our narrow kitchen, I stood in the doorway and explained my vague idea. I was going to fly to Berlin and start there. See what happened. I wanted to know if he had any recommendations, of places to go and things to see. I wanted to know what tips he could give me about the city of his birth, the place where he'd first understood the world around him.

Kneeling down on the linoleum floor between the washing machine and the sink, Pascal just shrugged. I'd be better off getting a guidebook, he said. Or looking on the internet. He was happy for me to use his computer.

That he did not like to talk about Germany back then I already knew; that he had little to say about Berlin or the other places of his family history. But I also knew that he had been back. That they had returned after the fall of the Wall to go to Berlin and travel on to the coast. He'd been with his father and he'd been alone. They'd gone to visit the friends and relations they had left behind when they moved to England. They even made one of those trips while we lived together, a visit to Hamburg where a cousin was getting married. Pascal drove, taking his mini down to Harwich and a ferry to Rotterdam, crossing north western Germany in an afternoon. He stayed two nights and was home barely 72 hours after he'd left, in no mood to stick around.

He spoke about those places like an outsider, I can see now, as holiday destinations he'd passed through but had not truly engaged with. Back then I don't think I listened well enough when we spoke to properly understand what was going on. I was too young and absorbed in my own plans and ideas to ponder on the strangeness of Pascal talking like this about the country of his birth; a place where he still maintained nationality, a passport and an identity card.

Berlin was okay, he said, coming into the living room from the kitchen, the washing machine already rumbling behind him. There were some cool bars and clubs, the last remnants of a scene that I was probably going to be too late to experience. I'd have to ask around when I got there. But if he was me, he continued, he would be travelling further than Berlin. He would go east, into Poland. Ukraine. Or south, to Bosnia. Montenegro. Berlin would be over soon, and it would be someplace else's turn next.

That night we went to the pub. It was late summer, and most of the students were still at home. We walked up into Headingley and easily found a seat in the beer garden. We drank beer and ate crisps, and Pascal was a little subdued. A few drinks in and he began to talk. He'd also made a decision, he said. While he was in Japan. He was going to give up the house. He had some jobs lined up, some assignments that would take him out of England until the new year. If this was to be his future, there was no need to keep the house. It was time to say goodbye to Leeds.

Maybe our paths would cross, he said. Maybe the next beers we would share would be on the banks of the Spree, the Vltava or the Drina, rather than the Otley Road. We drank a toast to this and continued drinking until darkness fell, and I was unsteady on my feet as we made our way home. Without the students around, the neighbourhood was quiet, and in my memory we were the only people walking the back streets that evening, still warm in the darkness, wearing only t-shirts, our jumpers tied around our waists. Back at the house Pascal got another beer and I poured a glass of water. We sat out on the front step. Pascal was quiet again, but I could see he was happy in the silence then, looking out across the rooftops to where the landscape fell away, down to the river, and the lights of Armley beyond, on the other side of the valley. We'd sat out there many times over the years I lived on Richmond Mount, and although I cannot be sure, I think that this was probably the final time we did it. A few days later I left Leeds for my parents' house in Lancashire, and as far as I know, Pascal spent the last month of his lease living in the big house alone.

On the plaza in Brussels I flick through the list of photographs I scribbled down on the first pages of my notebook, a mark next to the ones where Pascal has already recorded his thoughts. There is nothing that I can find that would give him cause to speak about those last weeks in Leeds. He'd taken a picture of his room on the day he moved in, and as far as I can tell, there wasn't another from the nine years that followed.

I don't remember the moment we actually said goodbye, most likely because it wouldn't have felt like a big deal at the time. It wouldn't have entered my head that I would only see Pascal for a couple of fleeting moments over the next fifteen years. I was simply going back to Mum and Dad's, as I had done so many times before.

The scene I have created for myself to fill the memory gap is that I would have packed the last of my things into a rucksack, before heading down the stairs that reached the ground floor between Pascal's room and the living room. He was still in bed, and so I knocked gently on the door. It opened quietly but it was enough to wake him. Pascal looked up from the bed with heavy eyes as I told him I was getting off. He nodded. He said he'd see me soon. And then he closed his eyes again and dropped back onto the pillow. Gently, I closed the door, and let myself out of the house for the final time.

It is possible that is how it went. It is also possible that he was sitting on the sofa watching television, or standing at the hob frying some eggs. He could have been sitting outside on the steps, with his first cigarette of the morning, willing the sun to finally breach the houses at the top of the hill. We don't always remember decisive moments of our lives because we don't always know they are decisive at the time. My original plan was to leave England for about three months. I was going to be home for Christmas. Eighteen years later and I have only ever been back as a visitor and, like Germany was for Pascal back then, England increasingly feels to me like a foreign country.

When we met in London on that hot summer evening three years ago, Pascal went into the pub to go to the toilet, and when he came back he asked me if I remembered the trip to Scarborough. There was a poster on the toilet door, he said. A nostalgic reprint of an old railways advertisement. Until he saw it, he'd completely forgotten that we'd made that trip. And until he mentioned it, so had I.

We went with Julie, one of our flatmates, who came up with the idea on a Saturday morning. It was a rare weekend when Pascal wasn't working, and so she suggested we should go for a drive. She just wanted to get out of our corner of the city, she said. To escape the collection of streets where we spent all of our days and nights. It was Pascal who suggested the sea and a road atlas told us the A64 would take us all the way to Scarborough. None of us knew anything about it apart from the song.

It began raining just past York and only stopped when we turned into Richmond Mount after we'd finally given up and gone home. In Scarborough, with the rain drumming on the roof, we'd parked the car by the park close to the Grand Hotel and made our way down onto the beach. There was nobody there apart from a couple of dog walkers braving the squall, and we trudged through the sand towards the harbour for no other reason than we couldn't think of anything else to do. At the other end of the beach Julie gave up, taking the car keys from Pascal and telling us she'd meet us there.

I followed Pascal as he walked out along the West Pier, towards the lighthouse where waves were breaking against the sea wall and sending spray high above the whitewashed buildings. Looking back across the sweep of the bay the town had nearly disappeared in mist that had rolled in. The Grand Hotel was a ghostly apparition, seemingly floating above the churning waters.

Pascal stood there for minutes, feet close to the edge as his trousers grew ever wetter with the rain and the spray from the waves. I held back for a while until I too decided to follow Jane to the shelter of the car. I put my hand on his shoulder and felt him give a start, as if he'd forgotten I was there. Didn't he want to come back to the car? Pascal turned to look at me, his face flushed from the wind, droplets of water running down his cheeks. I could taste the salt on my lips. I should wait for him there, he said. He wanted to stay a little while longer. Watching the water helped him think.

Outside the pub in London, Pascal sat back down on the step with a grin. It was some storm, he said. That day in Scarborough. If we hadn't been there and he hadn't had to drive us home, he could have spent hours just watching the waves.

In Brussels, the soldiers have dispersed. The two English men made their train. I have half an hour until mine leaves. The sun doesn't reach me now. The office blocks are too tall, and the plaza is in shadow. I finish my drink and gather up my things. I need to buy supplies for the train ride to come. It's going to be a long night before I see Berlin again in the morning. It's going to be a long night, and I don't think I will get much sleep.

*****

46

'On my last morning in Japan,' Pascal says, 'I walked out from the Ryokan and crossed the street. There was a wooden gateway by the side of the road. No pavement, just a little patch of gravel. A gate that led to a set of concrete steps dropping down through the forest. When we'd arrived in the minibus we'd been following the course of a river, with every twist and turn mirrored by the road above, and with my bedroom door open at night I'd been able to hear it, flowing down at the bottom of the gorge below. But I hadn't seen it. I wanted to see it. To know for sure.

The steps seemed to go on forever. I didn't count, but there must have been a hundred and fifty, maybe even two hundred, before I got down to the valley floor. The temperature dropped as I descended, and the air was damp. It was a place the sun never reached, the sides of the valley too steep, the gorge too deep. The kind of place that makes people go mad. The steps kept going down, down, down, until they reached a platform, where the river itself made a drop of about fifteen metres. A waterfall and a deep pool. Where the pool narrowed and the river raced off once more they'd built a viewing platform. It was a dead end.

I stood there for a while watching the water roll off the edge of the cliff. It seemed to hang there for a second, like a cartoon character, before it fell with a rush and a roar. The sound and spray was a constant, and you could feel the power of the waterfall even from metres away, on the other side of the pool. It was a power that had hollowed out the rock at the foot of the waterfall, so deep that even though the water was crystal clear it was impossible to see the bottom. It made me feel dizzy. The waterfall mesmerised me. To be honest, I have no idea how long I stood there, just watching and listening and feeling as the waterfall cascaded down.

At some point I was joined on the platform by a man. He was a bit older than me, dressed in jeans and a smart shirt. We smiled at each other but neither spoke. I searched in my brain for the words I'd picked up over the weeks I'd been in Japan, but none of them came. It was like the waterfall had erased my memory, and perhaps his too, because all we could do was stand and look at each other in silence for a while, both hopeful and frustrated at the same time.

He got there first. With another smile he told me in English that it was nice to meet me. Then he asked me where I was from. I told him, but it was only one answer, or one part of it. It wasn't the whole of it. I returned the question, and he simply pointed down at his feet. Here, he said. He was from here. I liked that certainty. And then he left, giving me a small wave from the bottom of the staircase, and soon he'd been swallowed by the forest. I stood a little while longer by the end of the pool, at that place where the sun never reached, until the thought of it made me shiver, and I followed him up the stairs through the trees, back to the world.'

Part Two

VIII.

A narrowboat cabin, in black and white. There is a bunk at one end, beneath a porthole, with two rumpled duvets and an open magazine, showing a double-page spread of a mountain panorama. At one end of the bed, a small shelf contains a row of books and a digital alarm clock showing the time as 10:07. There is light shining in through the window, so it is reasonable to assume this is morning. Next to the bed is a small set of drawers, built into the cabin walls. One is open, with clothes spilling out the top. Above, polished wood on which sit two beer bottles and an ashtray, two packets of cigarettes and a book of matches. The room is tight. At a guess, it is a little over two metres across, and the ceiling height is about the same.

'The houseboat,' Pascal says. 'This picture is a good example of the problem of photographs and their pleasure, when they are used as a way to remember. It is a pleasure because this photograph conjures up many happy memories. That was a happy time in my life and, when I look back, through this photo and all that it makes me think about, it makes me focus in on that houseboat and all that was connected to it. And that was a happy place for me, for sure. The problem is, I wonder what memories I am missing.

The more we look through these photographs, the more I am led to think about the idea that taking pictures and, perhaps more importantly, keeping pictures, leads to a hierarchy of memory. What you choose to document and store will eventually work its way into your subconscious. So I look at this photograph from the houseboat and certain things come right back to me, as if I was still standing there, my finger on the shutter button. They start a chain of thoughts, taking me beyond the houseboat, to other places and other times during those months, but the cabin is the start. The trigger. And it informs everything that comes next down the chain of memory.

The houseboat was in Stockholm. If it was possible to read the spines of the books by the bed you would see most of them are in Swedish. I was determined to learn the language and when I first arrived in the country I was convinced it was going to be easy. Written down it didn't seem all that far from German, and I was sure that within a couple of months I would be conversational, on my way to being fluent. And as I was staying for half a year, it was clear to me when I arrived that I would leave Stockholm with Swedish in my possession, one of the souvenirs of my time there.

It didn't work out that way. I went out, I met people. I attempted to talk to and listen to my students, outside of class. And I met Anna. But I soon realised it would be more difficult than I'd thought. My students preferred to speak to me about their work in English, rather than try to decipher my painful attempts at their language. I saw footballers on the television, halfway through their first season in the Swedish League, speaking it better than I ever could. And for Anna and I, we never reached that point. There was time enough, but as she said once, to someone I no longer remember, we started out in one language and that would always remain the basis of our relationship.

I don't know if I ever told you how Anna and I met. She was a friend of the person whose teaching I was covering for a semester while she was away in China taking photographs of villages that would soon be drowned by floodwaters raised with the building of a massive, hydroelectric dam. Anna's friend was called Linea, and we never met. In fact, her name and the story of the dam only just came back to me now as I am speaking.

Yes, Linea. She had left for China when I arrived in Sweden and she was not yet back when I departed for London. Anna came with me, but as you know, London didn't work for her and she soon went back to Stockholm. As for Linea, I can still picture her because she had a photograph of herself and another friend pinned to the fridge in the tiny kitchen on the houseboat. She had dark hair and big eyes. Her friend was male, with a round face and an untidy beard. They were in a photo booth, cuddled up together, and it looked to me as if that kind of closeness was normal between them. If Anna ever told me who he was, I don't remember now.

What else? I remember lying in that bed, only just a little bit wider than a single bed, holding Anna in my arms. I remember her telling me stories, catching me up on her life up to the point that we met. We would lie in bed with the skylight open, and hear people chatting on the path by the river. They were only a metre or so away but we would feel hidden, almost like we were spying on them. The weeping willow trees half-hid the houseboat, and I think most people presumed it to be empty. If they were speaking in Swedish, Anna would translate their conversations in a whisper. So often they said something that made us both giggle that I became convinced that she was making it all up. I didn't mind.

And I remember being in there alone, when Anna had gone back to her own flat or off to work in the morning when I had no classes, and the rain fell against the glass of the skylight above my head, and at that moment I was taken from the houseboat to another time and another place, so that now this photograph from Stockholm delivers me suddenly to a tent at Glastonbury, a campsite in Glencoe, to Norway once more... and so it goes.'

*****

The train moves through Belgium towards the border, and I follow its progress on the phone, as we pass between towns made famous by the beers that were brewed there. I know that I will have about five minutes to make my connection in Aachen, and any slowing of the train or lingering at one of the stops on the way takes me out of my concentration, and I have to move the recording back in case there was anything that I missed. When Pascal mentioned her name, it was the first time I thought of Anna since this project began, when really I should have been waiting for the moment that she appeared.

*****

'The best part about the houseboat,' Pascal says, 'apart from the time I spent there with Anna, was the drawbridge. It was really little, less than a metre in length. It rested on the gunwale, on the stone slabs of the embankment, and it was, when I think about it now, completely unnecessary. I could have stepped from the towpath onto the deck without any real difficulty, and Anna rarely came onboard that way, preferring to step from dry land the moment she came alongside the boat. But still, I liked that drawbridge for what it represented. It was a symbol, and the daily lowering and lifting marked my connection or not to the rest of the world. Each night I was deliberately separating myself, or Anna and I if she was there, from the mainland. From solid ground.

All the time I lived there I had these thoughts, daydreams that would eventually turn into sleeping dreams, in which I would lift anchor and simply sail away. Of course, I never did it. It wasn't my boat and I had no idea how to make it move. I'm not even sure if it had an engine. But still, I liked that thought, and Anna would play along, navigating us along the waterways, describing the places we'd see and the people we'd meet along the way. The rivers and the canals and the lakes, until we'd crossed the country and come out the other side.

Yes, I was happy there. That was a period when I was working a lot. I had my tiny flat in London but most of the time I wasn't there. Back then there were still good budgets, from magazines and newspaper supplements. Corporate work. Apart from those six months in Stockholm I was constantly moving for years. Stockholm was an anomaly, a period of peace and calm. Maybe I should have stayed. In another life, when Linea came home from China I moved into Anna's flat. I could have done my work from Stockholm. Maybe something else would have come up at the college. But in my memory there was no thought of this, no discussion. The time in Stockholm was fixed. The only question was whether Anna would come with me, and despite what happened, I'm glad she did. Because it means we tried. And if we try, we can have no regrets.'

*****

My fellow passengers are mostly commuters, travelling out from Brussels to the suburbs and outlying towns, a carriage of suits in dark colours, worn by men and women, of leather bags and laptops, and tired eyes staring through the window without looking. There's a shared sense of weariness on this train, and I wonder how many of them have their favourite seats and unspoken relationships with others in the carriage, and I wonder if I've unwittingly sat in someone's favourite spot, to add a further indignity to a long day.

Next to me is the only other person who looks like she is not on her way home from work, and I recognise her from the train before. Her name is Eva, and we speak in German, although she currently lives in Guildford where she studies acting. She's travelling home to Cologne and is also anxious about making the connection in Aachen. There should have been a direct train, she says, but the delays are getting worse each time she travels.

I have stopped listening to Pascal because it seems Eva is keen to talk, and she starts to tell me about her plans for the summer, of meeting up with old school friends she hasn't seen since Christmas. They will go to the lake and barbecue in her parents' garden, and she will enjoy the chance to exist in her mother tongue for a while. She asks me if I have the same, when

55

I go back to England, and I have to admit to her that half the time in Berlin I speak English anyway. She smiles and tells me there are no Germans in Guildford, or at least none that she knows. There might be an Austrian but, you know... She shrugs and smiles, and then wonders aloud whether her room will be how she left it. She is interested to know at what point we stop saying that we are going home when we visit our parents, and she looks at me expectantly, but I have no answer for her except that it does happen, that there is a point where we first become visitors, even if I cannot pinpoint it in my own memory, and that what applies to a house can also apply to a country.

*****

A room, shot from the corners, possibly from the doorway. To one side, against the side wall, is a desk with a computer and next to it a double bed. To the other side, a small kitchen unit. In between is an armchair and a coffee table, and a narrow, spiral staircase leading up and out of the picture. There is a poster on the wall above the bed, a black and white photograph of what looks like the ruin of a block of flats or perhaps a hotel. There is a sideboard, along which books are stacked, and a fireplace filled with plants. On the floor, in the front of the scene, is a bag, opened and with clothes spilling out, and a silver travel case, closed. Above the desk is a cork notice board, to which are pinned scraps of paper with handwritten notes, letters and postcards. Next to the computer is a mug, with a spoon resting in it.

*****

'The bedsit was advertised as a studio flat,' Pascal says, 'and it was really small. You can see almost all of it in the photograph, except the alcove with a wardrobe in it, the bathroom and the tiny room at the top of the staircase that led out onto a roof terrace. Ours was the only house in the block that used the roof in that way, and it was my favourite thing about the flat. When the weather was good, and the air was clear, you could see the towers of the city centre in one direction and the hills outside London in the other. I could see the planes taking off from City Airport and the DLR trains on their raised tracks, and it gave me a similar feeling to the houseboat in that, once I was up there, however claustrophobic the city was making me feel, escape was always possible.

This photograph was taken when I first moved in. The landlord lived in the rest of the house, and he seemed quite happy with me, probably because I was hardly ever there. He didn't seem all that bothered when I returned from Stockholm with Anna. He basically left me be, and I was fine with that. As I said, I was travelling a lot, sending myself postcards from the places I visited that would be waiting for me when I returned. It was the first thing Anna commented on when she moved in, the postcards to myself, pinned to the notice board. I don't know if she thought I was strange for doing this, but I remember she was disappointed when she realised I simply addressed them but otherwise left them blank. I could have sent a message to my future self, she said, and I had to tell her that it never occurred to me.

There were so many trips that there were way more postcards than those you can see in the photo. The rest were stored in a box beneath my desk, with all the old lenses and camera bodies that I no longer used but couldn't bear to throw away. The first things I ever consciously kept. Perhaps the only things, and yet I don't know where they are now, otherwise I would have sent some of the postcards to you. Or at least taken some pictures of them. Maybe they would have helped piece together the chronology of all those trips, if only through post office stamps. I have memories but I'm not sure of the order, at least in the early years when I was still shooting analogue. Afterwards, once I started in digital, it got easier. Everything is recorded.

I've only sent you rooms, but I was also looking for a picture from the roof terrace, and I don't seem to have one. That seems strange to me, but I've searched through all my hard drives and there doesn't seem to be anything there. I spent all those years recording these places, some of which meant so little to me, some of which I barely remember, and I missed that one place that meant so much to me?

Not many people ever saw that view while I lived there. You never made it to that flat, did you? After Anna left there were a few others, but not many. I'm not even a hundred percent sure I can remember their names. I don't think it matters. Ours are not stories that are mine to tell alone. It wouldn't be fair. With Anna, I don't know. Is it different? Do I tell our story? Perhaps it is enough to say that I loved her, and that our time together remains pure in my memory. I remember Stockholm and London, our nights out and our sitting up there on the terrace, watching the planes and the trains in the morning sun. Making plans for escape, plotting what we would do together, when we were still together. I've long stopped feeling sad that those plans came to nothing. It is enough to have had those moments. With Anna it was enough. We nearly made it. It is enough.'

IX.

The train slips across the border, leaving Belgium for Germany, with the Netherlands just out of sight behind some wooded hills. Almost immediately the train reaches the suburbs of Aachen, Charlemagne's city appearing soft in the evening sunlight. If Charles is waiting for me at the station to show me around his hometown there is no time. The Berlin train is already waiting on the opposite platform. I hurry across and climb aboard the final carriage, finding a pair of seats at the back of the train without any reservations. It is the perfect place to wait out the night. I don't expect to get much sleep. Further down the carriage, I see Eva find a seat on the aisle. She's only travelling as far as Cologne. The train is moving before I've got properly settled, the city of the Holy Roman Emperors already retreating in the haze of the evening. I take out my file of photographs once more, put on my headphones and open my notepad.

*****

A train compartment. Two bunks, the upper one made up with bedding, sheets and a pillow, the lower holding a collection of bags, both soft and hard cases, a tripod and a roll of cables. In the corner by the window is a mirror above a small sink. On the wall to the left a ladder hangs, held in place by a metal frame. A jacket hangs on a hook. Through the window it is possible to see the blurred shapes of what might be a pine forest, beneath the pale light of a morning sky.

'You know this,' Pascal says, 'and I know I am repeating myself, but it is important and this is the best place to put it on record. Of all the ways there are to travel, I love trains the most. I love them for what they are, for their rhythms and their movement, for the stories that can be written onboard, for the mix of public and private space, especially on night trains like this one, that you don't find anywhere else, except maybe ferries. I love trains for what they represent, for how they changed the world, how they changed the way we think about time and space. I love them because when you are on a train you are both part of a scene and apart from it. Attachment and detachment. A train captures the attention of all who are within sight and earshot of it. The people waiting at a level crossing. Those strolling on an embankment or working a field. Those whose gardens back on to the tracks. In the moment you pass on the train, you are part of that scene, and from within the train itself you get that glimpse, fleeting and incomplete, of all the lives that are lived up against the railway line.

A writer I once travelled with, on a small, narrow-gauge train somewhere in the Swiss Alps, told me that without the railways we would have no common European culture. Think of the writers who criss-crossed the continent once all our countries were linked into this network. The opera singers who travelled for performances. The people who used the railways to go on holiday, to travel to another country for the first time. World War I battlefields and vineyards in France. To the seaside or the mountains. From capital city to capital city. Understanding that the distances between us were not as great as we once thought.

And yet, I know.

I know that the railways, built from Liverpool to Manchester and then on and on until they reached Vladivostok, were a symbol of progress and communication, moving time and space in our imagination, but they were also the means upon which the mechanics of war changed. They moved troops and equipment; literal supply lines that ended in the trenches that would later be visited by those early package tourists. And later, those railway lines would also be used to transport people, all those men, women and children, loaded into cattle trucks and carried south and east to the camps where most would never emerge.

There is a sculpture in Berlin, the city where I was born. It's at Friedrichstraße station. You almost certainly know it. There's always a few drunks sitting there on a low window sill on the side of the station building, and in front is this sculpture, a memorial to two different but interlinked stories. One side tells the story of the Kindertransport, of the trains taking children to safety, beyond the border and across the water. The other side tells of other trains and other children, young people born in Berlin like I was, carried to their deaths on trains that left from Moabit and Grunewald, from the Anhalter Bahnhof. When we studied the Second World War at school in Southport, I never thought of these stories being connected to me. That the language we spoke at home linked me to those camps like a railway line stretching all the way from the Irish Sea to Auschwitz. And if I thought about it at all, I turned away. I pretended the link wasn't there. This wasn't my legacy. This wasn't my trauma. It belonged to someone else. Until I reached the point where I knew I couldn't turn away any more. But I've drifted from the point. It wasn't with this photograph. With this room, with this train. I still wasn't there yet.'

*****

Germany passes by outside my train window but Pascal and I aren't there yet. There are still other stories to tell. I pause the recording to scribble some further notes down, and then write four letters at the top of the page. Anna. She's been occupying my thoughts since Belgium, even as Pascal speaks of other things. I circle her name and then turn back to the photograph. Press play.

*****

'Friedrichstraße was later,' Pascal says, 'but I suppose you did ask me to record my thoughts as I look at these pictures, and this is where it took me. Where else? I know exactly which train I was on, but not exactly when the photo was taken. It could have been morning, but it could also have been evening or even the middle of the night. I do know that it was summer and that I was north, way north, beyond the Arctic Circle.

It was back during my time in Sweden. Anna and I took the train from Stockholm to Narvik, in Norway. There was no reason, except I had a few days off, I knew that the train existed and I thought I might be able to sell some photographs to pay for the trip. We went up there, right to the top, as Anna said, and then walked around for a few days. We wandered the streets and the port, and at some point went to bed, when our watches told us to. We watched the postal boats come and go and I climbed a hill from the edge of town that gave me a view of the fjord and the mountains around, some of which still had snow on their peaks. I left Anna behind, in the hotel room. She was sleeping.

For some reason I also left my camera in the room, and so all I have of that view from the hilltop is in my memory. I can still see the sailing boats below me in the marina. I remember trying to picture their journey north, trying to imagine what it was like to sail so far, hugging the coastline for many thousands of kilometres until you reached the top of the world. Just thinking about it gave me a kind of vertigo, even though the slopes of the hill were not that steep. I suddenly had this feeling that almost everything on the planet was beneath me. Every place I had ever been, every person I knew. Above me was just an empty space. I went down the hill and back to the hotel. In bed I held Anna so tightly that I woke her up, but I couldn't explain what was wrong. The next day we took the night train back south again.

The journey that was the thing. To leave home and get on a train that delivered us to beyond the Arctic Circle. To be taken further north than I have ever been, so far north that it made me dizzy. Is that not something? I remember sitting in that double compartment for hours, watching the scenery go by beyond the window. It barely seemed to change, but of course it did, only very slowly, imperceptibly. Trying to spot the shifts was like trying to catch the moment a child grows. Anna slept most of the way home, while I looked out of the window and failed to track the changes. I looked out the window and failed to track the changes and listened to her breathing above me. I can still hear her.'

*****

When Anna left London, Pascal called me in Berlin. It was one of the few telephone calls we had during those years, and I remember being surprised that he had my number. I had no memory of giving it to him. He called to tell me Anna had left. That he had just returned from the airport, where he'd put her on a plane to Stockholm. It hadn't worked out, he said, but he didn't sound sad. At least they'd tried.

About three months later I met Anna for the first time. She was in Berlin for a concert, and she sent us an email. She wasn't even sure if we had heard of her, she wrote, if Pascal had ever mentioned her name to us. Even if he had it might seem strange to only be meeting Sara and I now, but Pascal had always said that if she was ever in Berlin she should look us up. They had some time before the concert, and she would really like the chance to say hello.

We met her not far from the venue, in a cafe overlooking the river. The air was cool, but we sat outside so Anna could smoke as we drank hot chocolate against the chill in the air. She was in Berlin with some friends from home, but they'd gone to look at what was left of the Wall while she came to meet us. We spoke a little about who we were and what we did, and waited for someone to introduce the fourth member of our party who was absent, but very much there at the table with us.

In the end it was I who mentioned Pascal's name and then, deciding it was better to get things all out in the open, I told her that I was sad to have heard it hadn't worked out. She probably knew that Pascal wasn't really one for speaking deeply about his feelings, especially at such a distance, but that he had mentioned her often in our irregular contacts and that he had sounded so happy about everything.

Sometimes he was, Anna said. But it was never enough. He could never stop long enough. In Stockholm, tethered by his teaching work, they'd had a chance to make a start at something. But in London… She thought now that his constant moving, his restlessness and his inability to stay still was because he was looking for something. He was looking for a place to stop. For a reason. Anna thought that she might be the reason, and maybe Pascal did too. But after a few months in London it was clear that she wasn't. She wasn't enough. It was incredibly painful, Anna said, to realise it. Pascal argued against her. They fought. Nothing too bad, we shouldn't misunderstand her. They threw words at each other, not hands or fists. It hurt her to realise that Pascal did not see her as a reason. That she was not enough for him. She tried to hurt him back. But neither of them had it in them to hurt each other properly, so all they were left with was sadness.

He was searching for something, she said, as we shivered against the cold breeze blowing downstream with the river. She thought it might have been her. She said it again, as much to herself as to us. That she hadn't been foolish to think so. That they hadn't been foolish to try. But unlike Pascal, sitting alone on his terrace in London, watching the planes and the trains, Anna didn't sound convinced.

In Cologne I watch Eva walk down the platform, towards a couple who I take to be her parents. She's made it home. We catch each other's eye as the train slowly starts up again and she gives me a wave. The train crosses the Rhine in the long shadow of the cathedral towers. Only two days ago I sat on the cathedral steps, waiting for my connection to Brussels.

I think about how I will piece this journey back together later, in my future memories. The questions I will ask myself. When did I see the busker with the grey beard, one string missing from his guitar? On the way to London or on the way back? Which way was I heading when I caught a glimpse of Wuppertal's suspended monorail? On which train did I meet Eva? And was she reading the book without paragraphs, or was that another young woman living an actor's life in Guildford?

I read back the last few pages of my notes; Pascal's words, those that I have transcribed, and my own comments above and beneath them. Double-underlined for emphasis. Place names in block capitals. Stars in the margins. Months and years with question marks, attempting to understand the chronology. I have scribbled notes on the back of the photographs too, linked by code using numbers and letters to the scrawled words in my notebook.

There are plenty of pages left, and many photographs to come, but I know where Pascal is heading. All these rooms and all these stories, all these words Pascal speaks to me from his room on the island. The end point is already decided. What we're trying to work out together is how we got there, and how we can tell the story of the journey to the world.

X.

A twin room in what could be a hotel, a guesthouse or some kind of bed and breakfast. Both beds are made out of pale wood, as is the panelling on the walls. The beds have floral patterns on the duvet covers and pillow cases. There is no window in sight, but two paintings offer mountain views, the meadows in the foreground speckled with dandelions, daisies and buttercups while huge, snow-capped peaks rise at their back. Otherwise the room is bare. The bedside tables are empty, except for reading lamps with pale blue shades. It looks like the room is waiting; waiting for the next guests, the next people who will come to lay their heads.

'It was the first of my trips to Sarajevo,' Pascal says. 'This one was not long after we left Leeds and I had moved to London. I caught the bus in Zagreb and took it across the border, first into the Republika Srpska and then into the Federation of Bosnia and Herzegovina. That first trip was about six years after the Dayton Agreements, and it was possible to see the damage in the villages and the houses across the countryside. At one point in the journey we were even escorted by a white-painted military vehicle, soldiers hanging out of the back. I remember the bus falling quiet then, as if there was some unspoken danger that only passed when the soldiers disappeared, when we were able to drive on, unaccompanied.

It was dark when we arrived in Sarajevo. My guidebook said there was a hostel in an old train sleeping carriage, just around the back of the station. The station itself was brand new, polished and shiny, but I don't think there were any trains running yet. I found the trainyard and three security guards, sitting outside a portacabin around a fire that burned in a wide, metal bowl. It cracked and crackled as we attempted to understand each other. One of the men spoke some German, but looked bemused when I mentioned the hostel. He held my guidebook for a while, reading the entry over and over again, and then turned to look at the front cover, as if in search of the fool who had written such fictions.

He held his arms out. Look around, he said. There is no hostel here! No hotel or spa! Not even a pub! And his two friends chortled, as if to let me know that they'd understood everything that was going on the whole time. Then one of them reached into his pocket and pulled out a mobile phone. A Nokia. He dialled, spoke into it for a moment or two, and then looked up at me.

A friend is coming, he said, in English. And so I sat down with them on top of my bags and warmed my hands on the fire until Alex arrived about fifteen minutes later in his car.

Alex was not much older than I was, maybe in his mid-thirties at that point, and he owned a small guesthouse in the old centre of the city, not far from the market. It had been his father's, but his dad was old by then and, as Alex said as we drove through deserted streets, he had lost the knack of hospitality. Alex had only just returned to Sarajevo, having spent much of the previous decade in Canada, Sweden and, for a little while, in London. He'd been studying, working through an MA and a doctorate while the rest of his family were still living in a besieged city. By the time he told me this part of his story, we were sitting in the small reception area of the guesthouse, drinking beer from bottles he took from the fridge. I asked Alex how he felt about it, about being away while they'd all been here, but he wasn't interested in talking about it.

He hadn't come back to Sarajevo to live in the past, he said. The stories of war were not his stories. He would let those who lived those days have their say. They had suffered. They had earned it. A friend could show me around, if that was what I was interested in. Alex wasn't sure about it all, about this form of tourism, when the bodies had barely cooled and the wounds were still fresh. As he spoke I thought about my own plans. A photo series from Sarajevo and Mostar, from Croatia's Adriatic coast. The traces of a conflict. A story told in ruins. I didn't tell Alex. Instead I mumbled something about the beauty of the city and the surroundings. About having heard great things. Alex looked sceptical, but appeared to take me at face value.

I did meet Alex's friend, and he took me to the places where I could get the best photographs. I knew I would have no trouble selling them. People like to look at ruins. Since the Grand Tour, and probably before, we've been travelling great distances to look at the remains of Greek temples and Roman baths, the Abbeys long pillaged. We climb fences to photograph abandoned factories and tower blocks, finding beauty in emptiness and peeling wallpaper, in collapsed roofs and in decay. One photo essay would pay for my trip, that was what I was thinking in Sarajevo. It could take me away from sport and make my name as a serious photographer. The *Ruinenlust* of others. The desire to look at pictures of abandonment. *That* would pay the rent for another month.

Today I am sitting out the front of the house. From here I can see across to the town and the bay. At the end of the bay is an old tower. It might have been a lighthouse, or a watchtower. A place to keep sailors safe or to look out for enemies. It is jagged now, roofless and uneven at the top. Like a chipped tooth. You look at it and try to work out what forces led it to this state. Was it a war or some other cataclysmic event? Or was it simply rendered obsolete over time, by shifting economies or new technologies?

The fact is, it was built as a ruin. As a piece of decoration to complete the view of the bay. You'll find follies like this all over. A supposed mythical stone circle on an Irish hillside, built as a picnic spot by a Victorian landowner. A supposed watchtower at the head of a Scottish Loch, never used to watch over anything. Ready-made ruins because, in their decay, they've become timeless, become something rooted, and soon you forget that they haven't always been there, haven't always been part of the scene since time immemorial.

Alex's friend took me to the folded out remains of the old publishing house in Sarajevo. He showed me the shrapnel holes in buildings and on the pavement, filled with red paint. He showed me the gun emplacements high above the city and, on a drive into the countryside, an entire hamlet, gutted and abandoned. There was no poetry in these ruins. No Romantic aesthetic. Just the story of trauma and misery and all-too-recent loss.

I still took the pictures. Alex's friend, whose name is lost to me now, didn't disapprove. Some did, he said. Some members of his family didn't like how he made his living. A tour guide of misery. But he thought it important to share the stories. To tell people how it was. To show them what had happened. I remember, when I expressed doubts, that he just patted me on the shoulder and told me to keep taking my pictures and to show them. It was better, he said, than a fucking sunset. I told him I wasn't so sure. I'm still not.'

*****

The train moves through a Ruhrgebiet evening, the sun low behind a huge power station, billowing steam or smoke out into a violent-coloured sky. Here, former collieries and steelworks are UNESCO World Heritage sites, the Greek temples and Roman baths of the Industrial Revolution. New ruins of steel and stone, but also blood and bones. I rest my head against the window, still warm from the sinking sun, and close my eyes. I continue to listen.

*****

'Years later I went back,' Pascal says. 'To Sarajevo and Mostar, and down to Dubrovnik. The walled city was full of people, not interested in war or even the rugged beauty of the coastline, but a television show. Who am I to judge? The popularity would make it easier for me to sell my photographs, and as I think about it now, think about the decisions I made, about where I chose to aim my camera or which train I was going to take next, more often than not the decision was based on how easy it would be for me to get paid. I chased the ideas that might result in a cheque.

This is okay. It is the way our world is organised, the way it works. Or at least, it was until it wasn't, and photographs were everywhere and it became hard enough to be heard above all that noise, let alone get paid. More photographs were taken in one year than had been taken in all of history up to that point. As the volume increased, the value of what we did was falling through the floor.

Still, it is what I do and of course I didn't stop. But there was something about that later trip to Dubrovnik that led me to ask a few questions of myself. Was it simply enough to get paid? And was I getting paid enough? There was surely a better way to make a living, one that would allow me to take the photographs I wanted, rather than just those I thought I could sell.

I was down by the ferry port, where the boats arrive from and depart for Rijeka, Trieste and the islands. When I first came to Dubrovnik there was always a welcoming committee down there, a huddle of people offering rooms or apartments for rent. This time there was hardly anyone. The rooms and apartments were still for rent of course, just sold in a different way.

I started talking to a man who was waiting for his daughter to arrive on the ferry. She was coming down from Split for the summer and had decided to come by water, even though he'd told her it would be cheaper to go by bus. We had started to talk in English, but then switched to German when I realised he was more comfortable in that language. He'd lived for twenty years in Bielefeld, he said. He'd gone there to work and met his wife, who was from the north, up in Istria, but had also gone to Germany around the same time he did. They stayed long enough to build a real life, he said, to get married and buy a house. Their daughter was born there. I told him I was born in Berlin, but had moved away when I was young. He nodded and said his daughter had been six when they left for Croatia, and she did not remember much about Germany. To her, Bielefeld was a story. She wasn't even sure if it was real. It was a place of memory and of the imagination. It was fourteen years since they left, and they hadn't been back yet.

He had liked Germany, he continued, but it had always been clear they would return to Dubrovnik, although now it was getting so expensive, he wasn't sure if his daughter would be able to find a place to live when she finished her studies. She might have to move back into their house, and he was not sure she'd be happy with that. It was funny, the man said, but he had spent nearly two decades in Germany planning his return to Croatia, and now he looked at his daughter and the world that had opened up for her, and she was planning her escape. Maybe she'd even end up in Germany. Wouldn't that be something?

The boat arrived and the passengers disembarked. His daughter was one of the first, dragging two huge cases behind her. I watched my new friend hurry towards her, taking one case in each hand after they'd hugged a greeting. She was strikingly beautiful, taller than her father, with dark hair. Sunglasses on top of her head. She had a nice smile, one which she gave with her eyes as well as her mouth. In the excitement of her arrival he'd forgotten me, of course, and they walked off without a second glance. But he'd got me thinking.

That night at the guesthouse, sitting on the terrace beneath a canopy of vines and citrus plants, I thought about the man at the harbour, about exile and return, about comings and goings, the stories of families and the stories of places. It was then I had the idea for the Germany trip. To discover, and photograph, the places of my family and the stories I'd been told. That evening I sat up on the terrace and made a list, a kind of itinerary of all the places I would need to go. Places my parents had told me about. Places I'd read about in books. I didn't really know what I was looking for, except that it was an attempt to find my own Germany, my own connection to a place I'd long thought belonged to others.

I even wrote down Bielefeld, although I knew nothing about it except that it was the place where a man I'd met just a few hours before had once lived. I wrote it down and underlined it twice. I wanted to separate the places from the stories. I wanted to experience them first hand. I wanted to know if Bielefeld was real.'

XI.

A sofa bed in what looks like a living room. There are bookshelves on either side. A collection of plants on the floor. In front of the sofa bed, which is folded out and made with dark coloured bedding, is a coffee table on which sits a fruit bowl with two oranges in it. Above the sofa bed is a painting on the wall. A cityscape beyond an expanse of water. There are two figures swimming near the centre of the painting, only their heads above the surface, circled in orange in case there was any possibility of missing they were there.

'My father's flat, in Southport,' Pascal says. 'After mum died and I left for university, he sold our house by the dunes and moved into this flat on the first floor of a small complex not far from the station. It had a kitchen, a bedroom, a tiny study and the living room. I did not go and stay very often, but when I did, I slept in the living room in case he wanted to get up early and go to his study to work. This photograph was taken just before he moved to the island. I helped him pack the boxes. His thirty-five years in England were coming to an end. I was about to start the Germany project and I wanted to see him before it began. I think my idea was to ask him some questions, but when I got to Southport I knew that it wasn't the time. The decision to leave had come easy to him, but the process stirred up a lot of things in his head. He was quiet, thoughtful. It wasn't the right time, and I don't think I was ready either.

Being there stirred memories for me too. When I was a child, I remember being incredibly conscious of not wanting to be different. Of trying not to think of myself as different. It is why, when I think back to those days now, I learned English so fast. It was why I was quick to pick up the accent, that mix of Scouse and Lancastrian, to be commented on by the teachers at my very first parent's evening. In the beginning, if my parents spoke to me in German in front of my classmates I would refuse to answer. I would force them into speaking English. I remember saying, standing in the kitchen, barely as tall as the table where they sat, telling them that I was English now. In the Olympics, I rooted for the British athletes. In football, I cheered on England. Or Scotland, if Dalglish and Souness were playing.

It helped, I think, that in those early years there were two Germanys in my children's atlas of the world. Two flags. Two sets of letters in the medal table. FRG and GDR, West and East. If anyone at school did discover my background, the inevitable question would come. Which side are you from? And when I told them where we had come from, they looked at me as if I was from a science fiction film. An alien from another planet. After all, everything we learned was that the Wall was impenetrable. That people got shot trying to leave. How was it possible that we had come from there? My presence in a playground in northern England simply didn't compute.

It took me a long time to get from how it felt in that playground to the point where I was now ready to go back. To be planning those journeys to the country of my family. The place where I was born. The strange thing is, when I explained to friends of mine, in London or even old school friends I caught up with while I was staying in Southport, they seemed to understand it easier than I did. It was natural, surely, to want to know where you are from. Who do you think you are?

One friend said, as we nursed pints on Sunday afternoon in the pub, that we all like to think we're rooted somewhere, because otherwise we might just float away. I have always struggled with this idea, to be honest, because it seems to me to suggest that even after thirty-five years in England, having left

Germany as an eight year-old, that it was natural that I looked for history and a sense of belonging over there. That I couldn't possibly find it in England.

I'm not sure what I expected to come out of the process, when I made that rough plan in Dubrovnik and continued it back in London. I was interested in my family, of course, in the story of what it was that took us from one place to the next and then, in my father's case, his impending return as he reached his retirement. And I think I was also interested in discovering whether there was something in this notion of cultural heritage, a question whether, even though I'd been removed from it as an eight year old, there was still something that was a part of me. Would my soul stir in the shadow of the Lorelei? Would I feel the embrace of the German forest? Would I think differently, look at myself differently, after weeks and months living once again in my mother tongue?

And now, four years later, I ask myself the questions as I sit here, darkness beyond the window, and talk to you. What do you think, Ben? Did I find what I was looking for?'

*****

I'm on a night train without any beds, as it rushes through a darkness of my own. The lights are dimmed in the carriage, but a small spotlight above my head offers enough to allow me to make notes as I listen to Pascal talk. The strange coincidence of our friendship is that our childhood homes were only about fifteen miles apart. He was on the edge of the Irish Sea. I was in the middle of the cabbage and potato fields of the West Lancashire plain. He is six years older than me, but it is still possible that we might have passed on the pavement, when I took the train to Southport to buy school clothes or go and see the lights on the promenade. We walked the same dune paths as Pascal did with his mother, and we went to some of the same games at Anfield, usually midweek League Cup matches or, after the ban was lifted, the early rounds of European competitions, when tickets were easier to come by.

When we first realised this connection, back when I moved into the house in Leeds, it was an early building block of our friendship. We came from more or less the same place. We were castaways on the wrong side of the Pennines. When Lancashire came to play at the Headingley stadium, we'd walk over there to support our team, breaking cover as embedded agents deep in enemy territory, a red rose flag Pascal had rustled up from somewhere, hanging from the third floor window of the house on Richmond Mount.

*****

A hotel room. Double bed with heavy looking bedspread. Reading lamps with frilly shades. A desk with a bottle of mineral water, full, and a bottle of red wine, half empty. Through the window it is possible to see the hotel car park. The room is on the ground floor. Above the desk is a painting of a beach scene, with two women walking across the sands, white dresses blowing in the breeze, holding their shoes in their hands as they go. On the opposite wall, above the head of the bed, is a cross.

'The first place I went to was actually in France,' Pascal says. 'The second in Belgium. The third in Poland. In the exhibition, and in the book, the photographs from this part of the trip came later, in the bit where I was dealing with my family story. In my travels they came first.

For that first journey I rented a car and took the ferry from Dover to Calais. From there I drove south, past Arras and Reims. I arrived in Verdun without a place to stay, but found a hotel outside of town, close to the river. It was a kind of motel, a modern building beside a roundabout, with a small restaurant attached. If you stood at the window you could see beyond the car park to where the hills rose up from the bottom of the valley. In the bed, you could feel the vibrations every time a lorry passed on the street outside.

I started in France, in Verdun, because of my grandfather, my mother's father, who I had known as a young child. In the summers before we left for England we would visit him here on the island where I am today. My mother had grown up near here, in the face of the Baltic, as she used to say, calling this coastline home until she went away to university and met my father. We would drive up from Berlin and leave the car at the ferry port, as no vehicles are allowed on the island, and my grandfather would be waiting for us when the ferry arrived in the harbour. He was approaching eighty back then, but I never really thought of him as old. He was the one who took me walking up on the cliffs, or swimming in the lagoon. He seemed so fit, but after we left for England I never saw him again. My grandfather and my mum died within a year of each other. He was first. We learned about it by letter, sent from the island. One of his neighbours had found our address. Nobody in authority thought to inform us.

So I went to Verdun because I remembered my grandfather's stories. It was a place he'd told me about, a place in France where, he said, there had been a great battle. A horrible, desperate battle, one that went on for months. Hundreds of thousands of men died on both sides. The landscape cratered and ruined. It was impossible to imagine what it must have been like, my grandfather said, but there were those who survived and returned home and tried to explain. He was too young, my grandfather told me, but his older brother had gone off to fight. He would have been my Great Uncle, he said, but he didn't live much beyond his nineteenth birthday. He died in May, in a French bombardment, one of five thousand German soldiers who perished in three days of fighting.

My grandfather was fourteen when his brother died, at home in the port town of Swinemünde. The family learned of their loss via telegram. My grandfather could remember walking out

77

of the house when the news came, going down to the river where the fishermen were at their usual spot by the sea wall. It was hard, he said to me, to understand how something so terrible could be happening in France while it was so peaceful at home. He watched the river for a while and made a vow. When it was all over he would visit the place where his brother fell. And he did, many times. There was, he told me, all those years later, a part of his soul on those hillsides. He would go there to feel close to his brother once more.

I did the same. I wanted to visit this place that was so important to my grandfather, and so that morning, after breakfast in the hotel, I got in the car to drive up from the town and into the woods where most of the fighting took place. First I went to the memorial, a huge field of white crosses and the ossuary. My grandfather never discovered what happened to the remains of his brother, but there is a chance he is there, one of the 130,000 unidentified dead from both sides. I walked through the field of crosses and onto the terrace in front of the ossuary. It was quiet that morning. There were just a few cars in the car park, and one coach with a number plate from the Netherlands. I took some photographs and then stood there for a while, listening to the sound of the wind in the trees and the snatches of conversation carried over to me on the breeze, in French and German, Dutch and English.

From there I drove a little further into the forest, to the destroyed village. Fleury-devant-Douaumont. It is in the Zone Rouge, the area declared uninhabitable after the battle, and which remains so to this day. The streets are marked out among the trees, with stones on the ground to show what house would have once been standing there. A farm or a bakery. The school. A cafe. The ground is cratered, from the shells, and the only building in the village that exists today is the chapel. Rebuilt of course.

I stood there, in the heart of what had once been a village of four hundred people, and wondered if my Great Uncle had been one of those who had attacked it. Had he walked these village streets, where I now stood among the pine cones and moss-covered rocks? Had he seen the buildings in flames? As I walked back to my car, parked by the side of the road on the edge of the village, I saw a French family get out of their camper van, which was parked just behind me. The father nodded at me as I unlocked the car, and then he and his family followed the path I had just come up on.

I watched them go, sitting in the car by now but unable to leave. I was feeling shaky at this encounter, without really grasping why. After all, the father would have seen my British number plate. He knew nothing of my family story. And even if he had, even if he had known about my Great Uncle, well he was little more than a child at the time and it was a hundred years ago and... All these thoughts were echoing through my head as I sat there behind the wheel, unable to drive off, as the family walked down towards the chapel, the kids playing hide and seek among the trees as they went.'

*****

The train moves through the night, stopping every twenty minutes or so at another ghostly station. Who is catching this train in the early hours of the morning from Dortmund or Bochum, Hanover or Magdeburg? They stand on otherwise empty stations like apparitions. They are mostly men. They sink into their seats with a sigh, greeting those of their fellow passengers who are awake with a weak smile and a knowing look. We are a gang, fellow travellers, and it is easy to imagine we are the only train crossing the country tonight, the only people riding the rails while the rest of Germany sleeps.

*****

'I don't know how long I sat there,' Pascal says. 'I thought about my grandfather, and what he must have felt when he first went to that place in the 1920s, not much older than his brother had been when he was sent into battle. He never told me what the reaction was like in town when he got there, what the people of Verdun made of this young German coming to grieve his loss so soon after they'd been under attack and were grieving so many losses of their own. I know that he went there again, in the 1930s, and then again after the second war. It was his pilgrimage. There was a period of time when he was no longer able to visit France, but after retirement he was able to return to Verdun once more.

That final visit was not long before he told me the story, about this place he had only known in grief, that had been so important to him for almost sixty years. I remember sitting down by the lagoon, beneath the cliffs, as he talked to me. Not everyone would want to go there, he said. For some people, to visit the place where their brother died would be too painful. I could understand that, he said, even if I was young. But, he said, I should also know that to visit a place like this can be a reminder. It can tell you what there is to live for, and to live for those who didn't get the chance.

He was agitated as he told me this, as if he knew that his opportunities to speak to me, to share things with me, were already limited. It was important for me to remember, he said. He asked me if I thought I could remember. If I could keep it in my head, even after he was gone. It was only when I nodded that his face relaxed. That he seemed satisfied. He pulled himself up onto his feet and held out a hand for me. We had to get a move on, he said, otherwise we'd be late for dinner.'

XII.

I don't sleep. I listen to Pascal's voice and look out into the darkness. Certain stops on the line bring back memories. Of rainy days in a new city, climbing the steps of an old brewery to meet a friend. Of the World Cup and a long walk from the station to the stadium. Of visiting a brother-in-law in a town that seemed emptied of people, and a long lunch in a basement restaurant where we were the only customers.

It is the train, too. The rhythm and dimmed lights, returning me to a nighttime border crossing between Slovakia and Hungary, a dining car in Russia and a Trieste morning, mist hanging over the glassy Adriatic. I can see Rannoch Moor, dusted in snow, and the feeling of being in the middle of a blank space on the map. The train rattles and rolls. Sleeping heads shift in their seats. Backlit screens flicker, soundless. Scroll to the next file on the list. Ostend. Press play.

*****

'My grandfather walked to remember,' Pascal says. 'That's what he used to tell me. Which seemed strange to me, as a child, as he had chosen to live on this island, where his opportunities to walk were somewhat limited. It is about twelve kilometres long, which is enough for a decent wander, but after a while you'd be walking the same routes, time and again. I asked him, don't you get bored always following the same paths? I was reading adventure books, tales of climbing the North Face of Eiger or crossing the Sahara, and it seemed to me that taking the same path time and again was distinctly unadventurous. But I was missing the point, my grandfather said. It didn't matter that he always walked the same way, a six-kilometre loop from the house and across the fields, through town and then up onto the cliffs and the lighthouse. Every walk was different, he said, because every day was different. The weather. The flowers in bloom. The birds passing by overhead. There was always something new to see, something to discover.

And on the days when there was less to see, those were the days when he walked to remember. During the last summer I spent on the island, we followed his regular route together, across the field and through the town, up onto the cliffs. There's a point where the path runs down the back of the dunes, a wooden boardwalk around and beneath which the sands always seemed to be shifting, a permanent feature trying to maintain shape on a part of the island that was always moving. Walk the path enough times and you can sense it happening.

There was a particular smell in the air that day. Some flower or herb. It might have been lavender, or perhaps it was mint. It could have been the yellow rape fields that filled the island interior between the dunes and the lagoon. Or heather. Whatever it was, there was something in the air that took my grandfather away from the island. Today, he said, we were standing on the boardwalk, on the familiar old path. But part of him was far away, on a path behind a different set of dunes, just outside Ostend. In Belgium. I remember turning the word over in my mouth, as he began to tell me a story.

It was spring 1936, he said, and it was a long journey. He left his hometown of Swinemünde by boat, a short ferry ride to Stettin where he needed to visit the bank and a lawyer, to make some financial arrangements. I would learn, he said to me, behind the dunes on what was our final summer trip to the island, that if you want to leave the country there are some things you need to prepare in advance. Back then, what was important was to do what he could to move what he had to a

82

safer place. He knew, as the ferry crossed the lagoon to Stettin, that he might not be coming back. So he had to be careful.

We continued to walk and he ticked off the places he stopped off at on the way to Belgium, places I would later look up in my parents' old atlas at home, circling the names lightly in pencil so I wouldn't forget. Stettin and Berlin. Hamburg. Aachen. Brussels. It was more than forty years later when he told me this story, and he said that he did not remember much about the journey except for the sense of relief that he felt as the German border guards left the compartment in which he was sitting, to be replaced, moments later, by their Belgian counterparts.

He said goodbye, silently, as the footsteps of the two men retreated down the corridor, stiff in their uniforms of a country he had come to reject. He would only return once those uniforms were gone, hidden away in the back of wardrobes or burned in the garden ahead of the arrival of advancing armies, recognised for what my grandfather had known them to be a decade before. Symbols of shame.

Why Belgium? I think my head was still full of my adventure books when I asked him this question. You could go anywhere in the world, so why there? My grandfather just smiled and said that he had always loved Ostend, that it was a place he had visited many times after the first war. It was a place that gave him a sense of escape, and he described to me the wide promenade and the white houses overlooking the beach, the cafés and the bistros, and the sense, being there, of a permanent holiday. And he went there, I know now, because in 1936 that was where many of the exiles went. In Ostend that summer you could hear them talking in the cafes, sheltering from the sun beneath the heavy awnings, talking of little but the darkening days in the country they left behind, while in front of them was a carefree scene filled with colourful kites and sun umbrellas, ice cream stalls and brightly painted bathing huts.

My grandfather went to Ostend to buy himself some time, to work out what he was going to do next and also, I suspect, to grasp that sense of perpetual holiday one final time, an escape from a reality that he knew would soon intrude once more. Despite the length of the journey, reaching Ostend made him think once more about how small Europe was. As he watched the bartender take off the head of his late afternoon beer with a wooden spatula, only a few hours away people were being removed from their homes and placed into holding camps. Could it be possible that it was happening beneath the same sun?

Of course it was, but for a while my grandfather simply wanted to pretend that everything was normal. That he had not crossed that border into exile, but that he had just gone on holiday. It was impossible, though. He could not escape the stories filtering through.

The pretence was possible when he left the cafes and the hotel breakfast rooms behind, when he was outside beneath the sun and the blue sky, amongst the crowds thronged on the beach, paddling in the North Sea waves and strolling on the promenade. It was only as the summer came to a close, and the tourist season began to wind down, that his thoughts became more fixated on what was happening in the world beyond his holiday town. In Spain, it was already war. In Germany, it was coming. He could feel it. And he could no longer bear to sit for those long afternoons in the company of his fellow exiles, who seemed all the more visible at their café tables, now the rest of Ostend's visitors had returned home.

He had two choices, my grandfather remembered all those years later. He could join them at their table and drink to forget. Or he could walk. He decided to walk.'

*****

I try to picture Pascal and his grandfather, on a wooden boardwalk behind the dunes, the old man trying to help the child understand. A story from more than forty years before, recounted into my ears about forty years later. Could it be possible that all these details were so easily passed on and remembered, the layers of the story stacking up, from Ostend to the island to this train, racing through the night, in another century?

*****

'My grandfather walked to make plans,' Pascal says, 'to decide what should happen when his time in Ostend came to an end. And he walked to remember, to think about all those he had left behind. Just as there were parts of the island that, years later, would take him back to Belgium, there were places in Ostend, beyond the town and along the coast, that took him back to Usedom, the places of his childhood and his youth. He felt it among the dunes and the plantations of beech trees used to control them. He felt it in the wind, blowing in off the sea, and in the sand-scattered paving stones beneath his feet, and the sense that anything man-made was temporary, that if left long enough then the dunes and the beach would shift once more, claiming the territory back for themselves.

One day he walked to the French border. It was his longest walk during his time in Belgium, the longest, he would later guess, of his entire time in exile. He didn't set out to do the full forty-odd kilometres from Ostend to the border, he just went for a walk and kept walking, only stopping when he ran out of path in sight of a checkpoint. He walked for seven hours in the late summer sun, sheltered behind the dunes from the cooling breeze blowing in off the sea. Despite the warmth, he could smell the change in the seasons of the autumn that was about to come.

Seven hours from his hotel to the border. Arriving there in the middle of the afternoon. He spoke to one of the Belgian guards when he got there, asking him about transport back into town. The border guard asked him in return what he thought he was doing. Why had he walked all that way? Perhaps it is because my grandfather had no real answer that the border guard took pity on him, pulling over the next car that crossed over from France to insist that they gave him a lift to the next town where he could catch a bus back to Ostend.

My grandfather walked to remember. On the island, we had reached the point where the path starts to rise up from the dunes and onto the cliffs, where the lighthouse shines its warning to passing ships. I remember him telling me about Ostend and its harbour, about the boats and the women he met in the bars and cafés, although I was really too young to understand such things. We reached the top of the cliffs and for the first time the view opened out from the lagoon between the island and the mainland to encompass a sweep of the Baltic Sea.

It was still that day, glassy. The horizon was hazy, and it was impossible to see where the water ended and the sky began. He had realised in his life, my grandfather said, that he always needed to be close to the water, to be able to look out into the offing. My mother felt the same. These are the things we take with us.

My grandfather only ever went back to Ostend once, after the war. He was on his way to France, or maybe he was coming home. It wasn't important. By the time we were walking together on the island, he doubted if he would ever return. Not now. But it didn't matter. He walked to remember, and that allowed him to return. He could bring those places back, he said. They were carried on the breeze and in what he felt underfoot. And he could see them when he stood high on the cliffs, and looked out to the horizon, where the sea met the sky.'

*****

A hotel room. Double bed and mahogany desk. Double doors, open out onto a balcony, and outside it is raining. Beyond the balcony is a choppy sea, gunmetal grey like the sky. The wind has blown the curtains off to the side, obscuring the picture hanging on the wall.

'I went to Ostend,' Pascal says, 'but I find that now I have no real memory of it. When I look at this picture, all I can think of is my grandfather. My grandfather and the island, and how we walked and he remembered. I think of Ostend and I think of the island. Of the town itself, I can conjure up nothing except the feeling that in all the time I spent there, four days and three nights, it never stopped raining.'

*****

When I met Pascal in London on that hot summer evening, he was just about to leave for Verdun and Ostend, to start the travels that would take him to Germany. After Belgium he was to travel to Poland, to the town where his grandfather was born and lived before going into exile. From there he would come to Berlin. I offered him a room in our apartment, but he said he preferred to stay in a hotel. He didn't want to be in our way. He already knew where he was going to stay, in the west of the city, close to Ku'damm. He had stayed there before and he knew that he liked it, mainly because that part of Berlin felt so different to the city of his childhood. Sometimes it was good, he said, to be in a neutral space.

This conversation comes back to me now, and I wonder if he already knew he was ill when we met that day. I don't know and I'm not sure I will ask him. What I do know is that the Pascal who sat with me on the Kingsland Road feels more like the friend I lived with all those years ago in Leeds than the person speaking to me now through my headphones as I travel through the night. That Hamburg, six months ago, is somehow more of a dividing line. A chapter break.

Time stretches, time compresses. Sixth months feel like a lifetime. Eighteen years melt away. Before Hamburg, Pascal never once asked me if I remembered anything about our time together in Leeds, about our own story. It was not a game he was ever interested in playing. It feels a little different now.

XIII.

A t Magdeburg station the train stops long enough for some
of my fellow passengers to step out onto the platform and
light up a cigarette. None of them make it to the designated
smoking area, a painted square on the ground next to the bins.
The conductor smokes with them, the conspiracy of the long
distance traveller. There is no roof above the platform and the
smokers shiver in the dawn light until, one by one, they walk
over to drop their cigarette ends in the ashtray at the centre of
the painted square and make their way back to the train.

*****

Another set of open doors, another view of the sea. This time the
sun is shining and the horizon is a sharp line between the water
and the sky. Inside, the room is all shadows. A bed. A breakfast
bar. The outline of a fridge. Tiled floor and a rough-looking rug.
Black and white photographs in silver frames hang from the
walls and a towel hangs over the back of an armchair. On the
balcony table is a bottle of beer, Polish brand. A pair of shoes in
the doorway, half inside, half out. On the bed is a map, unfolded
and opened out on top of the covers.

'I could see Germany from my window,' Pascal says. 'It was the
resort part of Świnoujście, in one of the new apartment blocks
that look out across the dunes to the beach. My building was
the very last one, before the forest and then the border. On the
balcony I was higher than the trees and could see across the
dunes to the sweep of the bay and, in the distance, the piers

of Ahlbeck and Heringsdorf. The weather was so clear I could make out the cliffs of Rügen on the horizon. I spent a lot of time on that balcony, watching the ferry to Sweden come and go, spying tankers and other big ships at anchor offshore, and the flash of lights at the end of the sea wall.

When my grandfather lived there, the town was called Swinemünde and was part of Germany, although he had family members from both sides and grew up speaking both German and Polish. During the war, while my grandfather was in London, putting those languages to use in the service of British intelligence, the town was bombed heavily by the Americans. When I was a child, I was less interested in what happened to the town than I was in the fact that my grandfather was a spy. Or at least, that's how I imagined it, even if he told me that he spent the entire war working behind a desk. When the war was over, and Swinemünde had become Świnoujście, my grandfather left London for Greifswald, not far from where he'd grown up. He came to the GDR because he believed in building socialism in Germany. He went to Greifswald because he wanted to be close to the sea, close to Usedom. He got a job teaching languages at the university, and could spend weekends on the island of his childhood. Only the very eastern end was in Poland, but it meant his hometown was off limits.

Both his parents had died in the bombing raid of 12th March 1945. They were buried on the edge of town, in a cemetery at Golm, which after the borders were redrawn was part of the GDR while Świnoujście was in Poland, a town separated from its dead. This was what happened when men sit at meeting tables with maps and draw borders, my grandfather said to me when I was a child. We had a map open on the kitchen table at his house on the island. Someone decides, he said, with a stroke of the pen, that this is now Russia, this is now Poland, and this is now Germany. And then millions are forced to scramble, to find their place in the new order. Świnoujście was separated from its dead, but most of the people who called Swinemünde home were not. They'd also moved, and Golm was on their side of the border.

From Świnoujście I decided to walk to the cemetery, to where my great-grandparents were buried. It took me about an hour and a half. From the sea I walked inland, through the new developments of the past couple of decades, and the communist-era sanitoriums, the old German hotels and boarding houses. It was as if each block represented a different period in the city's history, which of course they did. I passed by the station, not far from where my grandfather's apartment house once stood. It had been destroyed in the bombing raid and replaced by a block of flats in the 1970s.

Eventually my route led me out of town, to a colony of allotment gardens, the smell of woodsmoke on the air, and then a brand new bicycle path that led me across an open expanse of marshland. In the middle was the border, marked with posts of red and white, and black-red-gold. On the other side, the land rose up to low, wooded hills. There used to be a lookout point there, a day trip destination from the town, with a view back across towards the harbour and a beer garden on the summit. Now it is a deathly quiet place. Trees and black crosses on the hillside. A concrete mother forever mourning her lost children.

I stayed for a long time. I took so many photographs. Of the beech trees and the crosses, walking back and forth across the slope to try and work out the pattern. But it was different to Verdun. There were no neat lines, there seemed to be no order to it all. Three, clustered together over there. Four, in a row, over here. Two sets of two, couples perhaps, down by the footpath. There were brass plaques listing the names, so many names. Polish and German. After the bombing the number of dead was so great that they had to pile the bodies onto wagons, pulled by horses through the still-smouldering streets.

Of course, I forgot. You've been there, haven't you? You told me when I came to Berlin. You knew the hillside, the view across town. The crosses and the beech trees. I meant to ask you whether there was anyone else at the cemetery when you visited, or if you had the place to yourself. For four days I returned to Golm, always walking from the apartment, through the town and the allotment colony, across the marshes. Three hours walking each day, back and forth to the cemetery, and in all the time I spent there, among the trees and the grave markers, I never met another person. Can that be possible? Have I blanked them out from my memory? Was there no one to come and pay their respects any more? Had all who survived now perished? Or had they been scattered too far, too old now to make the journey?

Each evening I ate in the same restaurant, on the main road, the street that leads from the border past the station and right down into the town centre. It was a nice place, with old furniture and old photographs, and a dour waitress who spoke German and never smiled, but somehow seemed to like me. I would walk to the cemetery, spend a few hours there, and then walk back via the port to the restaurant. On the way I would stop by the water, the little channel that separates Świnoujście from the rest of Poland, to the ferry to Trelleborg and the grey military boats, the coal barges and the heritage sailing ships.

Old men fished from the embankment as they had done when my grandfather was a boy and vowed to visit his brother's grave. And then I would go to the restaurant and wonder about the family of the waitress and my fellow customers, where they had come from now and in the distant past. I had spent too much time at the cemetery. It was shaping my thoughts about everything I saw when I wasn't there. I was walking through Świnoujście but not really, and yet I wasn't in Swinemünde either. I was somewhere in between.

I knew that I had to move on. After the fourth day in Golm I resolved to leave, and the next morning caught the boat to Szczecin, the same journey my grandfather took when he left for exile. From there I caught the train to Berlin, to cross the border over into Germany, and to come and see you.'

*****

I met Pascal in a cafe under the S-Bahn arches, close to Friedrichstraße station. He was full of energy, his food remaining mostly untouched as he talked, a torrent of thoughts turned into words after a couple of weeks spent in his own company. There was some nervousness too, I sensed, about his being in Berlin. Since 1989 he had been back to the city many times, but almost always for work and never for long. There had been one trip, with his father just after the Wall came down, when they searched out some of the haunts of the past, but never since.

*****

'The Berlin I had come to know on my visits to the city,' Pascal says, 'was to my mind a completely different place than the one we left behind in 1980. In my imagination, Berlin was two cities still. Not divided by the Wall, but by time, the Berlin of then and the Berlin of now. I don't think it's a coincidence that I created a new personal geography of the city on those visits, spending most of my time in the old West, sleeping in Charlottenburg, meeting friends in Kreuzberg. I only drifted East when there was a specific reason. An exhibition or a restaurant, a cinema or a party. And when I got there, I would find myself relieved if I didn't recognise a thing.'

*****

When Pascal came from Świnoujście though, he was looking. By the time we finished our meal in the restaurant beneath the S-Bahn arches, he was all talked out. The main focus of his conversation had not been Poland, or crossing the border to visit the cemetery, or Ostend or Verdun, but Sophie, the woman he'd left behind in London. They'd been seeing each other for about a year, and it was the first serious relationship since Anna had returned to Sweden. Somewhere in the file there is a photograph of her bedroom, but in all the recordings

Pascal hasn't mentioned it, or Sophie's name at all. She had been supposed to meet him in Berlin. The tickets were booked. But she never came.

We walked down from the restaurant to the river, following its course towards Museum Island and Alexanderplatz. The problem, Pascal said, was not that they didn't see a future for the relationship. They both did. It was just that the futures they saw were very different. At the time I think I just presumed it was Anna all over again, but maybe I misjudged him. Maybe I was just viewing Pascal as the man I'd always known. It is possible, when I recall the conversation now, that this time it was the other way around.

We ended up in a small bar close to Rosa-Luxemburg-Platz. A survivor from the 1990s. We had drifted there, not through any design, but because it is the part of the city I know best, a place where I knew we could get a quiet drink. I didn't think about Pascal, about his father and the Volksbühne theatre, about the plays his father had written and that had been performed there. I didn't think about the department store just down the road, where his mother worked. I didn't think about the fact we were just a couple of streets from where they had all lived, on the third floor of an apartment building that had been Pascal's first home. But though I knew some of this then, it did not come to me that evening. We all have our stories of the places we call home, and they are individual to us. I took us there that evening because it was the neighbourhood where I spent my first weeks and months in Berlin, not long after I'd said goodbye to Pascal in the house on Richmond Mount. I didn't think about the rest.

Perhaps it is because I only discovered what Pascal's father had been, before he was an academic in England, when I moved to Germany. It was only then I learned about the plays and the essays, the novel and the poetry. Very little had been translated into English, and even in Germany he had been mostly forgotten. In the bar by the theatre, Pascal wondered aloud whether any of the stagehands and actors drinking at the bar would know who his father even was. I told him I thought they would. After all, his books were all in print, and even if his plays were rarely staged any more, he was part of literary history. Surely they would know his name.

He asked me if I'd read his work and I told him about Sara's shelf above her desk, and the plays she'd studied at university. About how it was her who told me about my own friend's father and his life before England, before he stopped writing. Pascal had never told me any of this, although he insisted that the books had always been there. In Leeds and London. Some of the few belongings that moved with him.

We ordered another round of beer. He had never seen his father's plays performed, Pascal said, his voice soft. He'd read them all, of course, but he'd never seen them the way his father had envisaged them, as he sat at his desk in Berlin or in the small study at the house on the island during those long summer holidays. Pascal only had a few memories of him as a writer, he said. There was one time, during that last summer before they left for England, when Pascal was eight years old. His father had called him into the house from the garden. There was a scene his father was struggling with. One of the boys was about Pascal's age, and maybe he could help?

For fifteen minutes, Pascal said, looking into the top of his beer, they acted out the small scene. Back and forth. Back and forth. Years later, when Pascal looked it up, he could see the result of their work. It was his words on the page. He remembered his father asking, what would Pascal say in this situation? How would he react? His father scribbled notes on a pad of paper, notes that would be typed up, printed, and eventually spoken by a young boy on the stage. Pascal remembered his father holding the piece of paper up to the light that shone in from the window. The lines he had given him were perfect, his father said. Pascal was allowed to go back outside to the garden.

It was the last play he finished before they left for England. There were no more after that.

Between Brandenburg and Potsdam the mist hangs low over the flat fields of Berlin's hinterland. I'm almost home, the long night almost over. I will climb into bed next to Sara and sleep for a few hours, and she'll leave me there to begin her day as I reach the end of mine. Pascal has long fallen silent. Lost in thought, I hadn't noticed the recording come to an end. On my phone I write a message to him. I tell him that I'm almost back in Berlin. That I'll leave for the island in a couple of days. That I've made good progress on the recordings and that there are not many rooms left. That by the time we are together I'll be ready to begin.

I fall asleep for the first time as the train idles at Potsdam station, waking twenty minutes later as we approach Zoologischer Garten: the rain moving slowly between the apartment blocks of Charlottenburg, lifted above the city streets on raised tracks.

XIV.

Striped wallpaper, green and gold. All the furniture – the beds and the nightstand, the armchair and the table – is heavy and old. Green curtains on either side of the window, pulled back. No view, because there's a net drape, creating a bright white space at the centre of the image. Parquet floor, with wooden chevrons, and a rotary dial telephone on the table. Two beds, neither have been slept in. Although it is clearly daytime, all the lights are on.

Another hotel room. So many hotel rooms.

'It's on a side street of Ku'damm,' Pascal says. 'You know it. I've stayed there on most of my recent trips to Berlin. It used to be the residence of a silent movie star, back in the 1920s, and the owners keep the theme going throughout. The furniture. Photographs of the actor and her fellow stars. Artefacts from the period. As I say, I like it there because it offers me a different Berlin, a city that has nothing to do with the one that still exists in my fading childhood memories.

During those last few trips through Berlin I thought about my relationship to the city a lot. Although I was born there, I don't really consider myself to be a Berliner, and on that journey from Poland into Germany it felt not like I was continuing this search for my family's story, but that I was actually trying to leave that behind. I was trying to get a broader sense of Germany, which is why I changed my plans. I was originally going to go from Usedom to Greifswald, where my grandfather lived after the war, and then to Schwerin, my father's hometown. But instead I went to Berlin and then to Thuringia, to the Harz Mountains and then the Rhine. Bavaria. After Berlin, they were all places that had very little to do with my family's story.

It was the same during those two weeks in Berlin. I walked the Ku'damm to Halensee, down through Grunewald to Wannsee. I spent the best part of a fortnight exploring the west of the city, apart from the times I came to see you and we met down by Rosenthaler Platz. I knew that at some point I would need to deal with those places of my childhood, the places connected to my parents and their life in Berlin both before and after I was born, but as I say, I was trying to move beyond our story. After all, my grandfather's hometown was now in Poland. The country I was born in no longer exists. Those Germanies are gone. What remains?

I tried to speak and read only in German. I bought newspapers from the kiosk on the corner and read them in a café across the street from the hotel. There was a bookshop a short walk away, and so I bought slim volumes of poetry, the kind of texts I imagined I would have studied had we never left for England. I bought biographies and history books, piling them on the table in the hotel room, reading them long into the night. I was trying to catch up, trying to imagine and recreate what could have been on that school syllabus. I spent two weeks reading about the Thirty Years War and the Reformation. In that hotel room I walked the Harz mountains with Goethe and Heine and sat beneath North Sea skies with Lenz. I went to Carnival with Böll and the battlefield with Remarque. I watched old films on my laptop, some of which featured the star whose house I was staying in. I visited museums. Read plaques. Searched out memorials.

It was haphazard and, ultimately, I'm not sure what good it did, except to fill my head with the images of places it now felt important that I see. On a cheap road atlas I tried to sketch out a route.

I've lost the map now, but we can work it out from the photographs. All those hotel rooms, mostly interchangeable. How many do you think we should use, Ben? You said to me once, after Hamburg, that the images only had power if we could find a way to tell the stories connected to them. And that if there was no story, or the story was too personal, or not mine to tell, then we could pass it over. Not everything needs to be in the book. Not every story needs to be told. But now I'm looking at all these images from the trip, all these photographs from different hotel rooms in different parts of Germany, and they say nothing to me until I learn the name of the place where they were taken. Then a story might come to me, but I ask myself the question: do I even need these photographs at all?'

*****

I have no way of knowing this, but something about this recording tells me it is late. That it is dark outside Pascal's bedroom window, and that elsewhere in the house his father is sleeping. If the window is open, he might be able to hear the waves hitting the beach, but even if he can, they are not loud enough to find their way onto the recording. It's just Pascal's words, his breathing, and the deep, dense silence of the witching hour.

*****

'I've taken another picture now,' Pascal says, 'although I know I'm supposed to make a new file. It's from Boppard. You can find it. The queen-sized bed and the floral bedspread. The heavy velvet curtains and the polished furniture. A picture on the wall by a mediocre landscape painter. But when I picked it up out of the pile I could not place that room in the hotel or the town outside. I had to turn it over. Boppard. 16th May. And then I know, then I remember the basketball court by the river, and the barges on the Rhine. The pedestrian zone beneath my hotel room window, and the drunks spilling out onto the street at closing time. So I ask again: do we even need these photos at all? And if we don't need the pictures, what is the point of all this? What's my role? A confessional, spoken into a mobile phone for you to listen to, wherever you are?

Here, the next one. A modern hotel, owned by a French chain. This room, with its bed and desk, easy-clean surfaces and stain-resistant curtains. This could be literally anywhere in the world, but I turn it over and I see that I was in Eisenach. And so now I know that I am not in any of the other eight countries on five continents listed on the hotel company's website. But there is nothing in that photograph, apart from the knowledge of where it is taken, that will help me back to that footpath on the edge of town, the river gorge narrowing as I climbed so that at a certain point the rocky cliffs were almost touching each other above my head, the sky down to just a sliver. How do I get from those bedsheets, tucked in so tight, to that path above the town, a forester's track where the trees blocked all views until all of a sudden they didn't, and it no longer looked as if the forest was going to go on forever? What brings me from the laminated menu, in four languages, to the ramparts of the Wartburg and the room where Martin Luther chased away the Devil by throwing his inkpot at the wall?

It's late. My father is asleep. I should be asleep. My limbs ache and I have pain, but my head races. I've laid all these photographs out on the bed. We're getting close to the end. What do I have to say about them? What is there that you can use? That *we* can use? Let's just say that I travelled through Germany and took a lot of photographs. That they got me an exhibition and a book and a prize, that my friend went to London to collect, because there will be no more hotel rooms for a while. And while I travelled, and in between those photographs that won me a prize, I carried on this habit that I began when I was fourteen and that says what about my life? That I slept in many places? That mostly, I was sleeping alone?

Maybe that's it. Just put that in. In most of these rooms, he slept alone...'

*****

The recording continues for another forty-five seconds. It is possible to hear the sound of movement. The creak of furniture, a bed or a chair. The shuffle of papers.

*****

'Maybe we should just leave them all out,' Pascal says.

*****

At Zoo station I wait on the platform for the U9 to take me home. It is busy with early morning commuters. Smart clothes for the office. Jeans and leggings for school and college. It feels hectic after the calm of the train that carried me through the night, and I feel wired now, with a fear that I've reached the point where I won't be able to sleep. The U-Bahn train enters the station and the crowd tenses, pressing around me. The recording has stopped but there is one more in this file. I press play.

*****

'I'm sorry,' Pascal says. 'I managed to sleep for a while. At least, until the sun came up. I forgot to shut the curtain and the room floods with light really early, even though it is facing west. I sat at the window for a long time this morning. I watched the early fishermen out on the sea, their flags on long poles to mark where they drop the lobster pots. The sea was still then, but by nine the wind had picked up and the first of the sailing boats came out, racing the white horses across the bay. It is calming to watch them go back and forth, and from a distance I try and work out what the technique is. In my family, we like to talk about our connection to the water. To the sea. And yet I don't think any of us has ever learned how to sail.

I also listened back to what I recorded last night. I was going to delete it. To get the photographs out and try again. Because there were some interesting things that happened to me in those places, things that should be part of the story. In Detmold I went to see the Hermann Memorial, dedicated to the man who stopped the advance of the Roman Empire at this place among the trees in 9AD. The founding myth of the Germans, where the forest tribe defeated the mighty Romans. In Hamburg I walked through the brick warehouses by the old harbour and talked gentrification with the students I met in a bar by the station. In Weimar I walked from the statues of Goethe and Schiller until I reached the gates of Buchenwald.

And I realised, as I moved through Germany, that I had set myself an impossible task. It seems strange to say now, with the book and the award and everything, but I was never going to find what I was looking for. You don't carry with you a relationship to place, a sense of belonging, in your blood. And you can't replace it with book reading and a tourist trail journey through these sites of supposed collective memory. I was talking to my father about this the other morning. When I knew these photographs were coming up. He said that we are all who we imagine ourselves to be. Ideally at least. Sometimes we are who others imagine us to be. I guess that's the point where things start to get problematic.'

*****

In the tunnel, the U-Bahn train rattles along the tracks, the sound so loud that I can barely hear Pascal speaking. I turn up the volume, so that his soft voice drowns out the rest.

*****

'I took a boat on the Rhine,' Pascal says. 'A classic river cruise, with an open top deck and rows of white benches. A place to get sunburned while listening to Romantic poetry inelegantly delivered by the man who pours the beers between recitals. Of course, what we were all waiting for, as well as the beers, was *Die Lorelei*. Heinrich Heine.

> *Ich weiß nicht, was soll es bedeuten*
> *daß ich so traurig bin;*
> *ein Märchen aus alten Zeiten*
> *das kommt mir nicht aus dem Sinn.*

I'd read those words only a few weeks before in the Berlin hotel room, and when I saw the river cruise was going to take in the rocks where the mermaid sang the poor boatmen to their fate, I knew I had to go. The rocks themselves were underwhelming, and our boatman spoke the words with all the enthusiasm you'd imagine from someone who's been reciting the same lines, day in and day out, for years.

But then he said something interesting. Heine's poem, the boatman said, had been turned into one of the most popular songs of the 19th century, and it was so popular that when the Nazis later came to power, and had banned and burned Heine's other work, they still allowed these lyrics to survive. Even though they'd been written by this German-Jewish poet they continued to appear in collected anthologies, where they were listed as being written by an Unknown German Author. Even decades later, into the 1960s and 1970s, some of the boatman's colleagues were still crediting the work to an unknown German poet, long after the Nazis had been consumed by waves of their own making.

We are who we imagine ourselves to be. Sometimes we are defined by what others imagine us to be. After the boat had turned, beyond the rocks, and we were on our way back, I started talking to a couple who were sitting next to me on the bench on the top deck. They were from Flensburg, close to the Danish border, and she told me that she'd studied Heine in school and had always wanted to see the place where the Mermaid sang. She didn't seem disappointed, and why should she? The sun was shining. The beers were cold. We were all on holiday. Because they were friendly, and I hadn't really spoken to anyone since I was with you in Berlin, I told them what it was I was doing. They seemed interested, and thoughtful as well, in that way people are when they themselves have always felt so sure in who they are and have only just considered that there might be others who fall outside these realms of certainty.

When we got back to town we disembarked together and they both shook my hand. Then the husband said that he hoped I would find what I was looking for, but that I shouldn't get too disheartened if I didn't. As they walked away, I tried to work out what it was he was trying to say, between his words. Did he think that it was impossible? That I was too much of an outsider?

And then I thought of Heine. A man who lived most of his life in France, who had a complicated relationship with his own sense of who he was, and yet was able to write words that captured a national mood so well that even the Nazis allowed them to continue to echo around the rocks that stood guard over the Rhine waves. Perhaps the man was just telling me not to force it. After all, he hoped I would find what I was looking for. He was not telling me that I shouldn't even try.'

*****

At Leopoldplatz the U-Bahn empties. Two more stops.

*****

'When I laid the photographs on my bed again this morning,' Pascal says, 'I saw that the Rhine was near the end of my journey. From there I travelled north to Detmold, then to Hamburg, and back to Berlin. I didn't know it then, but I had started some kind of process. Do you remember what we spoke about? I think it started then, on the banks of the Rhine. It started after being in the shadow of the Lorelei. My soul did indeed stir, but perhaps not in the way that I thought it did, even at the time.

Look at all these rooms. I think that we should leave them all in. All these rooms, disconnected from the world outside. A procession of images that mean nothing. Banal. And yet, lined up one after the other in front of me on my bed, they do say something. Hotel room after hotel room. Hadn't that always been my dream? There were so many places during this trip more than any other where I could have stayed with people. With family. With friends. With you and Sara. And yet I always retreated to these rooms.

Yes, I think we should keep them. We should leave them all in.'

XV.

The U-Bahn arrives at Osloer Straße and I climb the stairs to the surface for the short walk alongside the morning traffic to our apartment. Outside the tax office smokers take their final drags before clocking into work, as the first of their customers arrive to take a number and a seat in the waiting room. Next door, patients slowly walk along gravel paths in the hospital gardens, alone or with their visitors, with breaks on wooden benches. The kiosk on the corner is preparing for the day, the kebab meat still wrapped in clingfilm on its spit as a delivery of drinks arrives, unloaded onto the pavement from an unmarked van. I walk with the steady stream of students, making their way from the station to the college campus that occupies a whole city block on the other side of the street.

I walk with the sense of security that comes with being at the centre of a familiar scene. I have made this short journey between the station and our apartment block so many times. To buy a newspaper from the corner shop or noodles and hot sauce from the Vietnamese grocery store. Coming home from a late night in the city or off the airport bus, from where it stops around the corner. I know that I won't make it across the street on one traffic light change, that I will have to wait on the central reservation between the traffic as the trams rumble by at five minute intervals and the poplar trees, taller than the six-storey buildings behind them, sway in the breeze. There's a fifty-fifty chance that my key will catch in the lock and I will have to take it out again. On the third floor window sill, one of my neighbours will have abandoned a beer bottle, half drunk, rather than take it into their own apartment as they finally make it home. By the time I reach the top floor I will be breathing heavily but not out of breath, not like when we first moved here, but that is ten years ago now and time can get you used to anything.

Pascal returned to Berlin at the end of his travels, and when he did I met him on the street in front of our apartment building so we could go for a drink. We went to a bar on the corner, a bare room of high tables and stools, lit by candles and low-wattage lamps. We sat at a table by the door and he told me about his journey, about some of the places he'd been and some of the photographs he had taken. He was in a thoughtful mood, but was sure he had something. A coherent story. He would be returning to London with what he came for.

We ordered a round of schnapps to go with our beers, a toast to his success, but his mood was not celebratory. The bartender brought our drinks to the table and waited until we'd finished the schnapps, to save herself another journey to pick up the empties. Once she had returned to the bar, Pascal showed me some of the photographs he'd already begun to work on, saved on his phone. Street scenes and cemeteries. Riverbanks and forests. Even in the places where there was nothing waiting for him, he said, he was making memories as he went. You bring things with you. You make a start. And when you go again, next time, alone or with others, there will be something there. It's the start of the process.

He laid the phone down on the table and looked around. He asked me about the bar. Was it a place that we came to often? I thought back to all the years we had lived on Osloer Straße. Aside from my childhood home, I have never lived anywhere longer. I remember doing the calculations in the bar, surprising myself with this information. Could it possibly be right? And in all that time, had I really only been to this bar on the corner four or five times? Was that enough to build a connection?

It was a start, Pascal replied. He told me I would remember this bar for those few nights, with Sara and now with him. Meeting friends. It would mean something, even if it was only something small. That was how it worked. That was how you made a connection. And so did he. It was like each book he read in his mother tongue. Each place he visited, memory he stored, added another layer of experience, of imagination. That had been the whole point of the journey.

He stopped talking. Our beers were nearly finished. I caught the bartender's eye and she brought over another round. Two more beers, two more schnapps. This time she left all the drinks on the table and moved away.

If he had achieved what he had set out to do, I said, why did he seem so subdued? Wasn't he pleased?

Pascal looked up to meet my gaze.

The problem was that his goal had been wrong from the beginning, he said. He picked up the schnapps glass and drank it down in one, eyes watering. He'd jumbled it up in his head, he continued, after a moment's pause. He'd tied two things together that didn't really belong. He thought he was coming to fill a hole, a gap that contained language and culture and history in all its forms, but that wasn't it. Or at least, if it was, it was only a tiny part.

He smiled at me now. A real smile, including his eyes.

Because his aim was off, he said. He'd been looking in the wrong place.

He looked at his phone, where the photos had been and which was now blank.

It was about his dad, he said. And his mum. And he was never going to find it where he'd been looking.

*****

A long room with high ceilings ends at a desk in the alcove of a bay window. The bed is on the floor. A futon, or maybe just a mattress, resting on the floorboards. There is a guitar on the bed and a pile of papers on the desk next to a typewriter. A sofa against the opposite wall, with a coffee table in front. The walls of the room are bare and it is possible to see that the wallpaper is puffy, peeling in places. The window frames are cracked, and dust floats in the shafts of sunlight coming in from the outside. The only other piece of visible furniture is a bookshelf next to the sofa, with six rows of books, almost uniform in size and predominantly hardback. At the end of the bed, a laundry basket is overflowing.

Everything is in black and white and the shades of grey in between.

'This is not my picture,' Pascal says. 'My father found it among the boxes when he first arrived on the island. He put it out for me, for when I got here. It was my first room, he said, although he thinks the photograph was actually taken around 1971, before I was born. It was the first apartment my parents shared, in Prenzlauer Berg, not that far from you in fact. The neighbourhood was a mess then. Coal-heated apartments in crumbling buildings. There was a piece of graffiti my mum used to tell me about, a message on a house not far from where they lived.

Ruinen schaffen ohne Waffen.

Making ruins without weapons. Instead they used neglect.

They both came to Berlin to study. My dad from Schwerin, my mum from Greifswald. She wanted to be a teacher and he was supposed to be an engineer. That plan didn't last long. He soon got involved with a literary crowd, writing poems and reading them in the backrooms of pubs. She had always been a singer, in the children's choir in Greifswald and at home with her parents. She went to those same pubs when she arrived in Berlin. Looking for a place to sing. Looking for others to sing with.

It was in one of those backroom events that they met. He'd done a reading and stayed around for the music. My mum and her friends played a lot of folk music then, inspired by Dylan and the German *Liedermacher*. She liked music that told stories. She always liked stories. It was why she wanted to be a teacher, a form of storytelling to help children learn, help them navigate their way through those important years of their life. I guess that is what first got her interested in my father, although she always said she skipped the poetry bits, and had arrived too late to hear him read. Instead it was him who noticed her. There was mischief in her voice when she sang, he once told me, and there was mischief in her eyes when he spoke to her later.

The idea of engineering was soon finished. My father had different dreams. Some of those first poems, refined through many readings in apartments and pubs, were eventually published in one of the literary journals. He gave up his studies and was invited to join the writers' union. He began to work on his first play. Around that time there were opportunities for my mother too. The band she played in were offered the chance to record an album. A record deal. But the producer wanted them to leave out one of the songs. It was one my mum had written.

The producer said that the lyrics might be problematic, and she asked him if someone had complained. Were they being censored? He assured her not, but that he had experience, built up over years. He was able to make a good guess, he told her, as to what might cause a problem and what might not. And why make a problem if you could avoid it? Change the lyrics. Drop the song. Sing something else.

My father told her to follow the producer's advice. After all, hadn't he taken on some edits when he was putting together his debut collection? Hadn't some poems failed to make the cut? And it was true, there were some poems that would only appear in later editions, those published in Frankfurt and Hamburg rather than Leipzig or Berlin. It was just part of the process. A small sacrifice, in order that the wider message be heard. But she refused.

There was a band meeting, in one of their apartments. She was outvoted. It was democratic. She said as much to my father when she came home. Everyone else agreed. Leave the song off the album. They could still play it live; reach the audience that way. They could record it later, once they had a name for themselves. Her bandmates had a point, my father told her. It was not that everything had to be done at once.'

*****

I let myself into the building and climb the stairs. In the apartment, Sara is sleeping, and so I go through to the kitchen and fill the kettle. The sun is already above the rooftops, reaching our balcony which faces the courtyard. I step out and let it warm my face as I wait for the water to boil. From beneath my feet come the sounds of our building starting to wake up.

*****

'My mother died before I was interested enough to ask her about these things,' Pascal says. 'I only know them through my father's memories, ones that he is attempting to conjure now, more than forty years later. He tells me that she couldn't face the idea of having to compromise her vision right at the start. At the very beginning of things. And if she already agreed then, how would she find the strength to resist later? What did that say about her vision, about her art? She wasn't like him. She wasn't willing to play the game. My father tells me this neutrally. There is no judgement in his voice, on the choices she made or those made by his younger self. They were all trying to find their way, trying to navigate, and what was right for him was clearly not right for her. It didn't stop them being right for each other. After that, she only sang for us, in our apartment, until we arrived in England and she joined a choir as a way to make friends.

She had been teaching for two years when she became pregnant with me. My father was one of the rising stars of the literary scene, with a play in production in Berlin and another that was due to be performed in Anklam and then Stralsund. He was in discussions with Dresden and Jena. When I was born we lived a little longer in that Prenzlauer Berg flat and then moved to Lichtenberg, to a new apartment close to the Zoo. By this time my grandfather had been allocated the summer house on the island, and we travelled north to the Baltic at least two times a year. I went to nursery and my mum went back to work. It was a good time, my father says now, a productive and comfortable time. They'd found their place within the system, and it wasn't a bad place to be.

As it would turn out, my father's compromises would not be enough to save him. Not when the sands shifted beneath his feet, and not after he'd signed that letter. He went back and forth when he was asked to show his support. It was my mum, he says now, who finally persuaded him to do it. At a certain point we all have to have a line, she said. It lies in a different place for each of us, but when we reach it, we have to decide once and for all what we are willing to live with. This had to be his line, she told him. These were their friends, asking for help. Inaction would be the same as betrayal. I was five years old and remember none of it. When my father speaks of it now, he tells me my mother was clear. He had to know that to sit on his hands would have consequences. That to stay silent was no longer enough.

He put his name to the paper. It would take another four years, but from the moment he signed they were subconsciously preparing to leave. Different things pushed them along the way. A moment came when my father, under contract with one of the main publishing houses, delivered the manuscript for his first novel. His editor called to tell him publication had been delayed. It was nothing to do with the book, but a problem of distribution. Supply lines. Things like that. His editor loved the book, of course. It was everything he'd hoped for. There were no major changes needed, and of course it was going to be published. But given the supply line situation, and the paper shortage, it would only be published in an extremely small print run. Surely my father could understand? Surely he had seen the economic situation with his own eyes? Surely he knew that everyone had to make sacrifices?

That night my father went back to the flat in Lichtenberg and told my mum that he thought they should leave. The feeling had been growing in her too. There had been whisperings in the school. The possibility of a transfer. There would be time for one more visit to the island, but what I didn't know at the time was that my parents had already made the application for an exit visa. My father's book, collected by some friends who had visited East Berlin for the day, had been published in Hamburg to good reviews. An English-language version of his second play was to be performed in Montreal. It was the latter that formed the basis for his application, for himself, his wife and their young son. Normally it would have been unlikely, but perhaps the publicity he was receiving beyond the GDR was what persuaded the authorities. Or maybe they just considered his presence more trouble than it was worth. Perhaps it was just easier to let us go.

They got the news that the application had been approved while we were still on the island that summer. It caused a huge fight with my grandfather. Didn't they understand what this meant? He kept asking them, over and again, as I listened from the hallway. Didn't they understand? And this back and forth continued until there was no more energy left, and all I could hear from my place behind the kitchen door was silence. I wanted to scream, to say that I didn't understand, but I stayed quiet instead and took myself off to bed.

What they all understood in their silence, and what I didn't as I lay awake in my bed above their heads, was that leaving might mean we never saw my grandfather again. And so it came to be.'

XVI.

I step back in from the balcony and pull my laptop out from my bag. I call up the project files. There is something that has been bothering me, even as I listen to Pascal talk. The black and white photograph of the apartment in Prenzlauer Berg is the last in the list. There are no more audio files linked to any of the photographs I have in my envelope. But there are more recordings to listen to. I pull the coffee jar down from the shelf and spoon it into my cup and then sit down at the table and call up his voice once more.

*****

'I suppose we will need a photograph of where I am now,' Pascal says. 'Perhaps you can take it when you get here. You will see it soon enough, this room of mine. Mum died before the Wall came down, so we never made it back to the island together, but in her passing it was as if my father took over her dream of return that she held with her through those years in England and made it his own, as if he owed it to her and her memory. I don't really want to speak too much about her death. I was fifteen. There are some parts that are vivid and others that are blurred. Like all memories, I suppose. It was sudden. There was no long goodbye. To this day, I still don't know if that was better or worse. There is no time to get ready for it, but there is also no build up of dread. You don't get to say goodbye, but you don't have to say goodbye. I don't know. I still don't know.

My grandfather died a year after her, which meant he never had to experience being forced to return his wooden house on the island to the original owners, who'd had it taken from them at the end of the war. My father made inquiries from England at the time, but it was never for sale. Perhaps that was for the best. It was a strange time for him, in those early years after reunification. There was a resurgence of interest in his work, even though he had published nothing in more than a decade, and he used the money to buy a plot of land on the island, one of the last in the village, at the point where the track turns to sand on its way through the dunes and onto the beach.

He took his time with it, his plot of land. He would travel to the island during the university holidays, staying in a hotel and going for long walks on the cliffs. He would inspect the plot and have half-hearted meetings with architects and builders, but he was in no rush. It was only as retirement grew near that he started to move. He owned the land for fifteen years before they started to build, and nearly twenty before he moved there full time. For the second time in his life he said goodbye to a place he had called home and went somewhere to start again, only in his mind it felt more like a return than a new beginning.

We had started to spend more time together then. After mum died it was difficult, and it wasn't that long until I left home for Leeds and my wandering life. Of course we were in contact. We spoke and we wrote. There were visits twice a year. But as I think I've told you, without my mum acting as the link between us, we found it hard to get beyond the surface level where we had existed since her death. I think now that we were scared to discover what lay beneath, and the longer it went on, the greater was the fear.'

*****

I think back to that night at the bar on the corner. Pascal with his beer and his schnapps. Searching for the real point of his journeys, criss-crossing the many Germanys of his family's history, trying to fill the gap. Maybe it was in those rooms all along?

'I went to the island when the house was nearly finished,' Pascal says. 'We walked from the hotel to look at the construction site, and then we took a walk up to my grandfather's old house on the edge of the woods, and from there to the cliffs and the lighthouse. We shared our memories and spoke of those people we'd held close and who were now gone, and even though I could see in his eyes, in his reactions, that some of his recollections were different to mine, he was kind enough not to say. My father, of all people, knows the importance of memory, and especially those stories we tell to ourselves.

The second time I visited was after the house was finished and my father had completed the move from his flat in Southport. A lot of his belongings were still packed away in boxes in the spare room. Some of them still are. It was after I'd finished the Germany trip, after we'd been together in Berlin, remember? Drinking in the bar on the corner. I took the train from Hauptbahnhof and there was a crowd of people there, all waiting for the train to the seaside. Expectation and excitement. Good times ahead. At Stralsund I got off the train and walked through the town to the harbour. I got a coffee from the bakery and watched the ferry approach across the sound, bringing passengers to the mainland before taking me across. That night, sitting in the garden, listening to the sea and the wind in the trees behind the house, I asked my father about those Berlin years. About his own childhood, and what he knew of my mother's.

He'd learned to love this place through her. Like her father, she was not a native of this island. This was no birthright. That the island is part of our life at all is linked to my grandfather's work for the Party and the favours called in. It's got nothing to do with deep roots. But, my father said, by the time he came back here it was enough. It was about what the island represented. The wind and the sea. The racing white horses. The memories of time spent together. As I look at the photographs we have, Ben, the ones I have sent you and the memories they have triggered, I have also seen what is missing. I cannot tell this story without the island, without this place. And you cannot help me tell this story without it. I cannot wait for you to see it.'

*****

In Hamburg, when Pascal asked for my help, I thought it was about his illness. About how time suddenly mattered now, and that it could no longer wait. But I am not sure this is true any more. Part of me thinks he already knew where he would end up. That like his father knew long before, the story was always leading back to the island.

*****

'I've been thinking a lot about the photographs...' Pascal says.

*****

I hear the first stirrings from the bedroom as the phone rings, cutting Pascal off in mid-sentence. The number is unknown and the voice at the other end of the line when I answer is deep. He asks if it is me he is speaking to, in German, before checking if the language is fine. I tell Pascal's father that it is fine, that he can use either language, but even as I say these words I have a dread feeling, deep in my stomach. He knows, Pascal's father continues, that I am due to come to the island in a couple of days, but he is calling to see if I can come sooner. His voice is calm, no wavering or shift in pitch, even as he tells me that time has suddenly become very short. He knows Pascal would like to see me, and he believes that I would like to see Pascal as well. He suggests that I should come quickly, as quickly as possible. As Sara opens the door with a tired smile I hear myself agreeing, telling Pascal's father that I will come right away. Sara's smile leaves her face as quickly as it came.

Is this it?

I don't have the words to answer her question, and so we stand in the kitchen as the sun streams in through the window and hold each other for a moment, before I start to move. I go through to the bedroom to exchange the clothes in my bag, while Sara sits down to call up train times on my laptop, still open on the kitchen table.

Part Three

XVII.

I take a shower, standing under the stream of water with my eyes closed, barely moving, feeling every muscle in my body. I've been awake for almost twenty-four hours now, save for a few snatches of sleep on the train, and I try to remember the last time I felt like this. It is a dream-like feeling, one that envelops me, felt in every limb and a kind of soft-focus through which I view the world around me. I remember this feeling and it comes back to me now laced with nostalgia, for those early days in Berlin when I would stay up past the last U-Bahn, committed now to having to wait for the first train at sunrise. It takes me to an airplane cabin at the end of a long haul flight, descending through blood red skies to land in the early morning of Johannesburg on a winter's day. It is the feeling of those long nights with Pascal, in another country, sitting in comfortable silence in our living room, waiting for the dawn.

In my tiredness I feel a dull sickness in the bottom of my stomach. My train north leaves in just over an hour. The fear is that we only have memories left.

We had so much time back then, and we didn't appreciate it. There were whole days in our week with no commitments, no work for Pascal and no classes for me, whole days that could lead into nights and the decision to hold on through, because there was nothing in the diary for tomorrow either. We would watch films in the living room, videos rented from the shop at the bottom of the hill or out of Pascal's collection, a mix of action and arthouse, depending on our mood. We stayed awake on caffeine or Jim Beam and coke, the spirits brought back from France by a housemate who made booze cruise runs across the channel from his parents' house in Poole. There was always a moment when the decision was made. When the time ticked over and what could have been the end of something became the start of something else.

It was our tradition that if we made it through the night, we would walk down into town at first light, following the Otley Road beyond the park and the university, over the underpass where the motorway lanes were mostly empty, waiting for the rush hour traffic to flow in from the towns and villages around the city. Pascal would bring his camera with him for these walks, to take pictures of streets that, with the early sunrise of a summer morning, were as empty as if under curfew or lockdown. It was usually as we lingered on the bridge above the underpass, the city centre before us, that the euphoria hit, a potent mix of tiredness and caffeine-drunkenness, combined with cool morning air and bright sunshine.

Everywhere looks better at first light, Pascal liked to say, from behind his camera. Everything is infused with the possibility of what might lie ahead. But I often wondered if it had more to do with how we approached it, coming as we did from the other side. Ours was not an arrival with the freshness of the new day, but the satisfied weariness of the long-distance traveller, ready to stake a claim. We were survivors. The possibilities were born out of that.

It was a feeling that could not last, and time would catch up with us in the corner booth of McDonald's, just after opening. The coffee was scalding hot and the soft drinks teeth-achingly sweet, and while they had seemed like a good idea only half an hour before, they landed heavy on uneasy stomachs. As we watched the city come to life beyond the window, all those buses and cars and pedestrians streaming down the hill along the same route we'd had to ourselves not long before, tiredness curled around us like a cloak. Later, as we moved against the stream on the top deck of a bus we had almost to ourselves, Pascal would fall asleep with his head against the window, camera on his lap, and I would struggle to wake him as the hill rose in front of us and we got ever closer to our stop.

The water streams down my back. In my head, I return to the bar in Hamburg. I sit on my stool and watch the trains as they pull into the platforms having passed through the tunnel beneath us. I can feel them. I can feel their vibrations through the stool and the table, gently shaking the glasses of beer. Pascal is on his way to the island. He had summoned me here, to this train shed under which pigeons roost, because he wants to ask me something.

In the moment, I presume he is on the way from London. What I don't know, and will not find out until later, is that he is in Hamburg to meet a doctor. There is a treatment. Experimental and expensive, with no guarantee. I don't know if Pascal ever learned the odds, if that was how it was presented to him. He never told me if he was given a percentage chance. I never wanted to ask him.

He pushes the folder across the table. Rough cardboard, recycled and solid. As he sips his beer I open it to look at the photographs. Some are prints from long ago, in a variety of sizes. Some he developed himself, others by the chemist on the high street. Some are newer prints, uniform in size, even if they depict scenes that are in some cases decades apart. Originals scanned but lost. Sent away to a digital printer, returned by post.

I'll be your ghostwriter, I repeat.

Pascal smiles, shakes his head.

I should tell the story the way I feel is right, he says. He has begun to record his thoughts and will start to send them over soon. He looks at his watch. My train will be here soon. We are running out of time. He tells me I should come to the island. He says these words as I gather up my things. I shouldn't leave it too long. The next words are left unspoken. I give him a look

123

that I hope tells him that I understand. That he doesn't need to say it. I feel my train before it appears on the platform. The vibrations. A shiver. We say goodbye with a promise to meet. The next time we see each other will be on the island.

On the train back to Berlin I look at the photographs for the first time. All the different rooms. Beds. Cupboards. Windows. Curtains. Books. Magazines. Desks. Carpets. Paintings. The words will follow. The words that will help me try and understand what all these pictures mean. Pascal's voice, straight into my head.

Sara drives me to Hauptbahnhof. The streets are busy, clogged by construction sites, but we make it in time. We say little on the way, both lost in our own thoughts. Time has become very short, Pascal's father said. As we pull up beside the taxi rank by the station entrance, Sara asks me if I have everything. I tell her that I do, but in truth I have no idea what it is that I need.

*****

'I've been thinking a lot about the photographs,' Pascal says. 'About this thing that I have been spending my days doing, this thing that I decided would be the way that I would explore and explain the world. The way that I would make my tiny mark. The click of the shutter button. A tiny fraction of time. Let the light in, close it off again. Wait and see what appears. What has been recorded.

When I took photographs of sportspeople, of the footballer shaping up to shoot or the basketball player in full flight, of the graceful runner or the powerful boxer, I always felt like I was trying to capture the essence of the activity or the moment of drama. I was about emotion, I think, so that when I got it right, the viewer could understand the drama or the emotion of the moment even if they had no idea who the athlete was, or the state of play, or even what was at stake in the moment of capture. I liked to think that if I'd done my job properly, if I'd caught the moment right, then the photograph wouldn't even need a caption. It would be a failure if words were needed. Just look at the photograph! It's all there! It was my own form of arrogance, I think now. I was hired to illustrate the words written by others, but deep down I was aiming beyond that. I was going to produce the image that would tell the story without any need for a paragraph or a caption or a headline. The photograph that made words redundant.

In the end, though, what I was actually doing was attempting to capture a moment that would always mean more to those invested in it than it did to the casual observer. Picture a line of players, running towards the camera. Moments before they stood together, arms around each other's shoulders, on the half-way line. They watch as their goalkeeper saves the decisive penalty in a shootout, and the photograph captures the moment the line breaks in joy. Anyone can understand the triumph that is written in their faces, the tiredness in their limbs that adrenalin is pushing forward for one last effort in this moment of sheer exhilaration. Suddenly they can sprint again, while their rivals collapse to the grass, off scene. All of us can understand this moment as we look at it. The photographer was waiting for it. Of course it can tell a story without any words. But only those who care as much as, or maybe even more than, the players, will really feel it.

Context is everything. Cup final versus pre-season friendly. Training run versus Olympic Games. A punch thrown in a points decision versus a knock-out blow.

Later, when I began to take pictures of places, when I was trying to tell a different type of story, I remained convinced that photographs could do something that words could not, but I also began to more fully understand the limitations. A photo could offer no answers, I started to think. It could explain quite well how something was, but was less good at explaining how something came to be. It was immediate, visceral and visual. That was its strength. We believe a crime is committed if there is photographic evidence far more than if we only have eyewitness testimony. But what the photograph cannot tell us is the why. It can only ever offer us part of the story.

I thought about this a lot as I travelled through Germany, trying to understand my own relationship with these places. Images alone would not do it. And then, later, as I started to gather together all these photographs of rooms, I knew that they would help me acknowledge certain staging posts, the beats of the story if you like, but that we would need something else to help explain, to help those who would later look, and those who were not invested in it, to see the whole picture.

Don't get the wrong idea, Ben. I have never been more convinced than I am in this moment as to the power and the importance of photography. Of what a photograph can do. After all, our lives and relationships with others are played out in images more now than ever before. We all walk around with cameras in our pockets at almost all times. Any moment, however out of the blue or surprising it is, can and will be documented. So you have to understand that this all feels like something of a cruel joke when I only now begin to work out exactly what it is that I would like to do with this medium. It is only now that I can look back and see clearly where I was going wrong.'

*****

From Hauptbahnhof the train travels for a while under the ground before emerging to climb high across a bridge rising up over the canal, with a view back across to the city centre and the television tower glowing in the morning sunshine.

*****

'I should not be so hard on myself,' Pascal says. 'I wasn't wrong in what I have been doing all these years. But I was still learning. I was so convinced of the power of the image that I always believed it to be in competition. But if we want to know the

126

story, we need to use all the tools that we have. It ultimately explains why the Germany project failed. Not as a work of art. I can see that it spoke to people. I saw and felt their reactions. But in what it was supposed to do for me. And even now, as I look at the photographs of all these rooms, as I try to flesh out those beats of the story, I know that there is something missing.

In the past couple of days I have been taking photographs again. I was out yesterday, in the garden. I just used my phone. More than a hundred images. I was always learning, and I still have a good eye. Some of the photos are beautiful. Others are poignant. Some are banal. But the question is, what's the caption?

A Lazy Day in the Garden?
Island Living?
Narrowing Horizons?
Exercise Yard?'

*****

On the train my fellow passengers appear to be on their way to the lakes north of the city, making the most of this good weather. The mood is light in the carriage, a gentle buzz of conversation that I can hear as Pascal stops talking and the recording reaches an end. It is just over three hours to Stralsund and I know I need to sleep, but although my limbs ache and there's a dull throbbing in my head I don't want to close my eyes right now. Time has become short, and I still have work to do before I see Pascal again.

XVIII.

My last email from Pascal arrived in my inbox two days ago and with it the last of the audio files. There are no photographs left, he wrote. There are rooms vital to the story, for which there are no pictures. When he first had the idea, back before we even met in Hamburg to talk about it, he had thought there might still be time to revisit some of those places, to search out old photographs taken by others or to make new ones himself. He even thought about whether he should make new images look old. He had the skills, and who would know. More importantly, he wrote, would it even matter? The place would still be authentic, and the memories too.

In his words I can hear the enthusiasm for this idea, for a piece of trickery that will now never happen, and I can feel it drain away again as I read the next couple of lines.

He will just have to do the best that he can, he writes, with the words that come into his head. It is the only way he has left to travel, the only way he can conjure images of those missing rooms, of those old places that he knew now were so important.

*****

'A child's room,' Pascal says. 'Bunk beds against the wall. A desk beneath the window. There are football posters. A team in brand new kits that seem to glow in summer sunshine like the green of the pitch beneath their feet. Another picture, this time of a single player, identified as Pierre Littbarski, running with his arms aloft in celebration. Playmobil toys, scattered across the floor. The two bunk beds are unmade, and at the foot of the bottom bunk is a pile of dirty clothes that never seems to get any smaller, but no bigger either.'

'My Aunt was always trying to get us to tidy up,' Pascal says. 'She was my father's sister, older by a couple of years. She left for West Germany in early 1961, just a couple of months before the Berlin Wall was built. Tens of thousands left in those days. She tried to get my dad to go with her, but he was too young really. They didn't see each other for a long time. My Aunt was nervous about returning to Berlin for a visit, even with her West German papers, and the rest of the family was nervous about what her visit might mean for them.

She ended up in Cologne, where she met her husband. He worked at the brewery and she became a teacher's assistant. They had enough money to build a house, on the edge of the city, where they brought up their three children, my cousins. Before we moved into that house I had only met my cousins once, when they finally decided to come to Berlin, about a year or so before we ourselves left. Perhaps the adults on both sides had decided there was no more damage left to do. Not once my father had signed that letter.

We met them outside Friedrichstraße station and then took the tram. Ice cream in the park, that my Uncle insisted on paying for. I remember the discussion. My father telling his brother-in-law that we had enough money. My Uncle, holding his hands up in apology. That wasn't what he had meant. He knew my father was a successful writer. That we had money. It was just that he had been forced to change all these Marks. How else was he going to spend it? I remember thinking that he should just give it to me.

After we left Berlin we went to Cologne to stay with them while we waited for the British visas to come through. My father already had the job offer, and we were told it was just a formality. There was never any question of staying in Germany. My mum agreed. I remember the moment she told me that we were going to England. She called it starting again. We would learn a new language and make new friends, she said. We would have a house by the sea. You were never far from the sea in England. It was better, she said, to be running towards something than away from something.

In Cologne I played football in the garden with Johannes, the cousin whose room I was sharing. He was bigger than me, and better at football, but I think they must have told him to look after me as he tended to let me score a couple of goals. It was a shame we weren't sticking around, he said. They needed new players for the local team. Johannes was convinced he was going to become a professional, and had mapped out his whole career in a notebook in his bedroom. He showed me, one night after the lights were supposed to be out. He shone his torch on the notebook. First he would break into the 1.FC Köln first team, then he would sign for Real Madrid.

He passed the notebook and the torch up to me on the top bunk. There were lists, going on for pages, of each season in his imaginary career. He knew them off by heart and could explain in detail what was happening as I followed on the paper. In some seasons his team did well, finished high in the league or won trophies. Some seasons would be more difficult, especially when he was struggling with injury. Sometimes he would play on the losing side in the cup final. Against Bayern or Liverpool. It had to be realistic, Johannes said. Nobody wins all the time.

Still, by the time we reached the end of the list and Johannes was nearing retirement, there was nothing he hadn't won. And as he returned to his hometown club for one last hurrah, his goals brought the Bundesliga title back to the Rhine. In time, he was sure they would build a statue that would rival even Cologne's famous cathedral.

Johannes sells cars now. He still plays in a veteran's team for his village club. He rides a BMW motorbike to the match and leaves it in the car park when he's had too many beers. Sometimes we write to each other, just catching up. There have been more messages recently. I wanted to ask him about his room, the one we shared for those weeks before we moved to England. I was sure that he was on the bottom bunk and I had the top, but he said it was the other way round. He told me that I was afraid to sleep on the top, in case I fell out in the night. Because I'd seen it happen. And when he wrote it, I knew my memory had been faulty, and that he was correct. I hadn't wanted to sleep on the top because of Marienfelde. Because of what I heard and what I saw in the aftermath of the fall. The blood on the linoleum floor.

Pierre Littbarski was correct though, he wrote. Even for that year when he went to Paris, long after we'd moved on to England, Johannes had kept the poster on his wall. He was upset about his hero leaving, but he thought that if he kept the picture up there, still in his Cologne colours, then it might bring him back. It worked. Littbarski was only in Paris for one season before he came home. The faith had been justified.'

*****

The train moves through the Mecklenburg lake district, sun catching on the tiny waves of the lakes that appear here and there between the trees that line the side of the tracks. For a time Sara talked of moving here, to a small house by a lake. I tried to explain why it didn't work, because of our jobs and money and responsibilities we had in Berlin, and she told me I was missing the point. There were different forms of escape, she said. Sometimes it didn't matter if you actually did it. All that mattered was the dream, that it was possible. In that way, in your head, you were already there. Now she dreams not of a house by the lake but of the south. Of the land beyond the Alps. Soft light and warm air. She can already speak French, and has just started to learn Italian. As long as it is possible.

*****

'A long, thin room with small windows,' Pascal says. 'Bunk beds, like in a youth hostel. Two wardrobes. A fire safety notice on the wall. Linoleum on the floor.'

'We were not in Marienfelde for long,' Pascal says. 'Once my father received the exit visas we took the train from Friedrichstraße to West Berlin, travelling south to the refugee reception centre where we had to be processed before we could go on to West Germany. The officials knew my father, or knew of him at least, and he was treated like something of a celebrity. Nevertheless, we had to share our dormitory with one other family. They were a couple from Saxony and their daughter Mathilde. She was five years old. It was Mathilde who insisted on sleeping on the top bunk, and it was Mathilde who fell off in the middle of the night. Blood on the floor. She had to go to hospital for stitches, but she was okay in the end. After that they moved the Saxon family to a room of their own, and we had the dorm to ourselves.

I was only nine. I don't think it really registered to me that, when we walked down from the reception centre to the playground, we were still in the same city that I'd lived in all my life. That I was looking up at the same clouds, feeling the same breeze, sheltering from the same rain, that I would have seen and felt and sheltered from if we'd never left. For me, West Berlin was a wholly different place. And even though everyone still sounded like us when they spoke, I knew they were different. I couldn't tell you what it was, but I just knew.

My father would travel up to Zoo station to meet his publishers, who were disappointed in him for his plans to go to England. Surely a writer should stay in a place where he was surrounded by the language in which he was going to write? With hindsight, maybe they were correct. We'll never know, but at the time my father told them he was sure that he could not write what it was that he wanted to without distance. He felt that he needed to take his memories, he told me later, to a place where they could be preserved, untainted and uninformed by those places like West Berlin or Cologne that were both so familiar and so strange.

That was his plan. He thought he would land in England with his version of Germany in place and preserved, a resource he could mine without it being corrupted. It didn't work. If he wrote anything during his years in England, aside from the odd academic paper, it was never published. When I ask him now he says that he thinks such things can work in one of two ways. He'd hoped for one, but had got the other. There were many like him, he says now. They struggled for a subject. Before, he had never had to consider what it was he was writing about. What he was writing against. But by leaving it all behind, all the things he wrote about and wrote against, he found himself suddenly in limbo. He wasn't close enough. The publishers had been right. He wasn't close enough to his subject, to the subtle changes in behaviours and language that happen over time, the things that would allow him to write authentically.

I asked him why he hadn't then written about England. About Southport. After all, he lived there for three decades. He had tried, he said, but it hadn't worked. He wasn't ready. But I know that he is writing now, so maybe the time has finally come.'

*****

We are nearing the coast. Through the train window I've seen the first gulls circling above fields of yellow rape shining brightly beneath the sun. What clouds there were have scuttled away now, the sky an expanse of seemingly endless blue. I try to spot the city as we get near, ticking down to our arrival time. I try to spy the spires of the churches as we approach, the red-brick Gothic towers, the hulking blue of the shipyard and the high bridge lifting up from the mainland to link it to the island of Rügen beyond. I've seen them before and I know that they are there, but today it seems like Stralsund is hiding from me, out of sight even as the train is slowing for the station. It is only then, at what feels like the last minute, do the first buildings of the city show themselves.

*****

'I don't remember much about how my mother was during those weeks in West Berlin and then Cologne,' Pascal says. 'She was happy, I think, to have left it all behind. I'm not sure how comfortable she felt in the house of her sister-in-law. After all, they barely knew each other. And I remember her going out a lot, to the phone box down by the doctors' surgery, where she would make a phone call back across the border to my grandfather. He could have come with us, of course. It was more than possible. He was retired, allowed to travel. Held in high regard. But when he was asked, then and later, he said simply that he'd done enough travelling in his life. He was where he was and that was where he'd stay.

I was only nine, and so I didn't understand a lot of what was going on, but it felt back then and I am sure of it now, that my mum was experiencing something like grief or a deep, painful sense of loss. She knew there was a good chance that she would never see her father again. She walked to the phone box to maintain a connection, even though she knew there would be others listening to the call. It didn't really matter. She had nothing to say that would be of interest to them. It was just important to keep hearing the sound of her father's voice, however distant he might now be.

As for me, the weeks in West Berlin coincided with school holidays, so I only went back to class once we were in Cologne, once we'd flown out from Tegel having been processed by every department in Marienfelde. We collected stamps from the Germans, the Americans, the British and the French, and once they were satisfied that we were who we said we were, we were allowed to leave for West Germany.

Perhaps because it was the summer it took a little while, and we waited out the process at the local open-air swimming pool.

My father took me, sitting on his own with a book beneath a tree while I played in the water. I made friends with some of the other boys who were there most days as well, and I enjoyed the reaction I got when I told them I was also from Berlin, but from over there. They would look me up and down, as if there should be some identifying mark that I was missing, and that they couldn't believe that I was just like them. We even had the same brand of swimming trunks.

During the summer in West Berlin I didn't think much about what we'd left behind. It still felt like a holiday. I was missing the island, of course, because that was where we'd normally have been, but I wasn't thinking yet about the apartment or school, or my friends from the neighbourhood. But I do remember thinking, as the plane took off from Tegel, that I could see down across the border, into Prenzlauer Berg and towards Alexanderplatz, Lichtenberg in the distance.

I remember mum asking me what I could see. I told her that I could see all of Berlin. The whole city. I even thought I could see our apartment block, over there in the distance. I asked her if she wanted to look, offering her the chance to lean across me to the window, but she just shook her head and returned to the book that was open on her lap in front of her. In my memory, though, the book stayed open on the same page for a long time during the journey, at least until after the stewardesses had moved through the cabin offering drinks, and we were already flying through West German airspace.'

XIX.

I am following him. I am following Pascal on the journey he made six weeks ago, from Berlin to Stralsund and then onto the ferry for the journey across the sound to the island. He'd been to Hamburg once more, for a final course of treatment, and was on his way back. In Berlin he stayed over with us, and for the first time he slept in our apartment. I met him at the tram stop on the corner, and we walked home together. When I saw him step down from the tram it was impossible to know that there was anything wrong. He insisted on carrying his bag, and although he told me on the way that he was finding he got tired more easily than before, he climbed the five flights of stairs to our apartment without pausing, or even being noticeably out of breath.

He sat with Sara on the balcony while I cooked us a meal. Chicken and rice. It was late winter, and cold, but they both put on their heavy jackets so Pascal could smoke a cigarette. I watched him through the window as I cooked. He leant back in his chair, while he smoked and listened to Sara as she talked, watching her all the time. He laughed and said something in return. I couldn't hear either of them speak, but I heard his laugh, echoing around our courtyard.

They came inside to eat and we talked of nothing I can really remember now, although I do remember thinking how strange it was that this was the first time he had been in our apartment, he'd sat in our front room at the big table, surrounded by all of our things. And I remember thinking that despite that, it wasn't strange to have him there, and it was like he came to visit all the time.

After we'd eaten, Sara took the dishes through to the kitchen and didn't return. Pascal poured another glass of wine for us each, not stopping until the bottle was empty.

This was it, he said, smiling with his eyes as he looked at me. When he got back to the island the next day, it would be the end of his final journey. I think I asked him how he could be sure, but he just shrugged and then took a sip of wine, closing his eyes as he did. He couldn't be sure, he said, still looking into the darkness. It was hard for him to explain, but he felt it. He just did. The next morning he would take the last long journey and he would have that feeling as he always did on the train, that sense that he had felt so many times before when he was in motion: that time had somehow stopped, and that if the train could roll on forever, well...

He paused. Opened his eyes.

He wasn't sad, he said softly. He wasn't angry. The train could never roll forever. There was always an end of the line.

The next morning I walked with him to the station for the train north. As we waited on the platform he told me to take care. He put his arm around my shoulder. I couldn't find the words to repeat it back to him, so I just nodded. He would see me on the island soon, he said, and that he would be sending more recordings to me in the next few days. There was so much to say, and more that he wanted to record. There would be time enough for that. I asked him what else he would do when he got back to the island. He lifted his bag onto his shoulder as the train slowed to a stop in front of us.

He would go to the fridge, he said, and he would take out a bottle of beer. Then he would sit on the terrace, light a cigarette, and look out across the dunes to the sea.

*****

'I am sad,' Pascal says. 'But most of all I am angry. Does any of this feel fair to you, Ben?'

*****

At Stralsund station I send two messages. One to Pascal and one to his father. In both I ask the same question. Is there anything I can pick up for them in town. I still have some time before the ferry to the island, and I am more than happy to go to the shops. It's a normal question. The polite thing to do. I receive no answer.

*****

'My room in my grandfather's house,' Pascal says, 'was small, up underneath the roof. For most of the year it was the store, where my grandfather kept his older fishing equipment and the big travel chests full of all those things he wished to keep close but did not need around him every single day. There were also some boxes that belonged to my parents, things that were safer there than they would be in Berlin. For our summer visits he would clear a corner for my mattress, and a small table and lamp. There was a skylight, installed so the chimney sweep could get onto the roof, and from where I lay it was possible to see up and out to the stars. A ladder linked me through the floor to the rest of the house, and during the time we stayed there, I was the only one who ever went up there. It was my private place. It was my favourite room.'

*****

In Berlin, during one of his visits for the Germany project, I walked with Pascal through Prenzlauer Berg until we reached the street where his parents had lived when he was a baby. It was not far from the park, and when I first came to Berlin there were still houses in this neighbourhood that bore bullethole scars in their facades, courtesy of the Red Army half a century before. Now the scars were gone, smoothed away with new

138

plasterwork and paint, balconies bolted onto the outsides to catch the morning sun. We stood for a while in front of the building, looking up at what had been the bay window of their main room. Pascal had spent the first night home from a hospital ward sleeping beneath that window. Did he want to ring the doorbell, ask if we could take a look?

Pascal looked up for a little while longer and then shook his head. There was nothing here, he said, and turned to walk away down the street.

*****

'It feels like I have more memories of this island than I do of Berlin,' Pascal says. 'Maybe it is because I am here now. I might not move far from the house, but the memories come to me, carried on the Baltic breeze perhaps, or in the scent of the flowers growing on the edge of the garden. I never thought I could be attached to a place. I didn't think I had it in me. Anna always said that I fought it. Maybe she was right. But being here for the last few months I start to understand why my grandfather felt happy here. Why, at a certain point, he felt no need to leave. At some point in our lives it is time to stop moving. Don't you agree? I never thought I did. I dreamed of a never-ending parade of hotel rooms. Not so much now.

I remember, one day near the end of our final visit before we moved to England, talking to my grandfather about our leaving. It was around Easter, an unusual time for us to visit, but my father needed to collect some things from the boxes in the attic, and my mother wanted to say a proper goodbye to her father. Although we travelled up there at a different time of year to normal, there was no mention of our reason for visiting. Perhaps the adults had spoken of it during the evenings, when I was already in bed, but I hadn't heard it discussed or noticed the conspiracy of silence around it.

I went for the normal walk with my grandfather, and as we made our way across the fields towards the town, I told him all that had been told to me, back in Berlin. I told him we were waiting for our papers but they would soon be with us, and when we had them all we would take the train to the other side of Berlin. We would be refugees, like you sometimes saw on the news, and we would go to a special place to stay. Then we would see my cousins before we flew to England. Step by step it had been explained to me, so that nothing would come as a surprise, and so I explained it to my grandfather. Step by step.

He listened without saying anything, and once I was finished we continued along the track in silence. It was a good minute or two before he began to speak. Did I know, he said, that he too had been a refugee? That he had ended up living far from the place where he'd been born and brought up? It was a different situation, of course, but there were some things he wanted to tell me. That there might be a time when people would make fun of me. Or say that I didn't belong. They might tell me to go home, or just to go away, because people can be sad and be angry, especially about things they cannot control.

What I had to remember, he said, was that I was just another in a long line. Europe was a continent of refugees, he said. People had been moving, back and forth, for centuries. For love or for work, because of religion or war, or simply because they wanted to feel the sun on their backs or see the northern lights. It had always been that way. Humans were nomads. We liked to move. If life didn't work in one place, then surely it was natural to try for another? For a place where life might be better? What I didn't know then was that my mum had asked him to come with us. That he had said no. That he had told her his own moving days were done.

He had an uncle, he continued, who had gone to America. Before my grandfather was even born. Perhaps he had children, and they were as old as my grandfather was, sharing a name but living in Philadelphia or New York, San Francisco or Chicago. Maybe even Berlin. There was a Berlin in America. Hamburg too. The point was, we were all scattered to the winds, he said.

Who knew where we would land. Where we would put down roots.'

*****

Leaving Stralsund station I walk from the new town on one side of the ponds to the old city that curls around the harbour with its view across the straits to Rügen and down the sound towards the open sea. I follow a map on my phone that takes me through a square filled with parked cars and along a pedestrianised shopping street with its mix of architectural styles and a parade of shops similar to those found on equivalent streets in Berlin. At the next square I stop to look up at the distinctive gable end of the town hall building, as Pascal told me to do, and then duck down an alleyway towards the harbour.

There are plenty of people about, down by the water. Early beers at bars with a terrace and view to Rügen. Tourists milling around on the cobbled quay beneath the red-brick warehouses, looking at the old sailing boats or making their way over to the huge modern aquarium that shines bright among the rust-coloured brickwork of the buildings on either side.

There are two bridges between Stralsund and the island of Rügen. An old causeway, built in the 1930s, and the newer bridge that soars above it. Before either were built, the only way across was by a ferry that gave its name to villages on the water's edge. Pascal's island has no bridge. The ferry remains the only option. I stand at the edge of the quayside and look out in the direction of the island. I cannot see it, but I know that it is over there, lying low against the horizon, hiding from the rest of the world.

*****

'When we left for England,' Pascal says, 'we knew that we might never see him again. That we might never take the ferry to the island, to have him waiting for us on the quayside, as he had been all morning. And it turned out to be true that our

141

goodbyes that Easter were the final ones, in person at least. But I think he would have been happy to know that at least my father and I made it back here. That this place he found and fell in love with became so special to us too. And it makes me happy, Ben, that you will soon be here with me. That you will see our island. I have recorded the stories and sent them to you. When you get here, we can talk of other things. Just don't take too long.'

*****

At the harbour I buy a smoked fish roll from a kiosk by the ferry terminal, where there is already a gathering of people waiting to board. Most look like they are about to embark on an expedition, with their luggage piled up at their feet, ready for the summer holiday. I try to picture Pascal and his parents, having taken the same train north as I did, walking through Stralsund to catch the ferry to where his grandfather would be waiting on the pier. And the more recent journeys, of Pascal alone, knowing his father would be waiting for him in almost exactly the same place.

I think of all the photographs in my bag, all those hundreds of rooms Pascal captured with his camera, and the fact that not one of them is from the island, this place that that eventually pulled him back.

There is a low murmur through the crowd as the ferry appears through the haze. All the passengers are out on deck, watching for the skyline of Stralsund as it grows larger. Gulls fly off the back, above the waves churned up by the ferry's engine and which roll out to break gently against the harbour wall. On my phone I flick through my list of files. There are still a few left to be opened. The journey is almost over, but Pascal still has something more to say.

XX.

' It's midnight,' Pascal says. 'I managed to get up from the bed, and now I'm sitting at the window. I can see out, down the garden to the dunes. Beyond is only darkness, except for lights on the boats anchored offshore. There are apps that could tell me what is out there. Where they are from and what they are carrying. Where they are heading to next. But sometimes I think it is better not to know, to leave something to the imagination.

I was thinking of calling you, Ben, but I didn't want to disturb you or Sara if you are already sleeping. And at this point, a missed call in the middle of the night would only have you worried. We still have some time.

I've been thinking, trying to work out how best to do this bit, now that we've reached the last of the photographs. I still have some things I want to say. It's not even about the rooms any more, but about here. About the island. I guess this is where we were leading all along. But it's hard. Before, with the photographs, I had something to lean on. It all came easy. Now I have to rely purely on memory and it's more difficult. More painful. For what those memories contain, for what I pushed away so long, and what is now pulled from the depths of my brain. And then there are those I cannot access, however much I try.

I'm too tired, Ben. But I want to get these thoughts out. If you use them or not, well, that's a question for you alone. You can use them all however you wish. And if you decide not to, I'm sure my father would be happy to hear the stories that remain. After all, he's the last of us left.'

Close your eyes and listen to the gulls, a mother says to her daughter. The girl is sitting on the low wall, next to me. If you want to listen to something carefully, you need to close your eyes. Shut down the other senses. Concentrate on one.

Should you try and close your nose, too?

Her mother laughs while the little girl, with her eyes closed, clasps her nose shut with her fingers. Listens.

'When I first sat down at the window,' Pascal says, 'there were no stars visible. The sky and sea were just one patch of darkness. But now some of the clouds have cleared, and the moon is at three-quarter size, and I can see stars and gentle waves on the water where everything above is reflected below. All the lights in the house are out, and my eyes are getting used to what is out there, beyond the window. I can see the boats now, silhouetted on the horizon, and the grass on the dunes, blowing in the breeze.

We have a book downstairs. It's about eighty pages long and is printed on glossy paper. It is more pictures than words, with the name of the island on the front in shiny letters to catch the sun on the display outside the souvenir stall. And that's what it is, because it's not a guidebook, not really. It's aimed at those who have come here for a holiday and want to take something back with them. A souvenir of their trip, with photographs taken with more skill than they themselves can manage, and in better weather and at the ideal time of the day. The lighthouse is luminous white. The sands are golden. The trees are beautiful green against the brilliant blue sky. There are aerial shots, showing the cliffs at the northern end and the sand banks that, when viewed from above, seem to be bleeding into the Baltic water. There are pictures of the marina, the old fishing boats and the restaurants. Heather in autumn. Snow in winter.

Anglers in the shallows, horse riders on the heath and cyclists on the path behind the dunes. There are short texts on history and culture, the flora and fauna, the geology and the climate. There are useful phone numbers, long out of date, and a list of writers and artists for whom this place was an influence. My father's name is not there, but perhaps one day it might be, in a future edition.

The book was a present from the builder when he finished the house. He knew nothing about our long connection to the island, about our family history, and my father didn't tell him. The builder did know who my father was though, and had brought with him copies of books and plays for my father to sign. They looked suspiciously new, my father said. Unread. But that was okay. Some people just don't like to read. And even for those who do, there are more words than can ever be read in one person's lifetime.

When my father built this house I asked him if he was ever worried about being lonely here. The last house on the lane on an island at the very edge of the country. But he said he was never lonely as long as he had a view, and from the house you can see the trees in the forest and the sea and the sky, and from the kitchen window it's possible to look down the lane and see the cyclists ride, unsteady on borrowed bikes. I believe him when he says he hasn't felt lonely here. He also says that, at the same time, he is more than happy for me to be there with him.'

*****

I think of Pascal back in Yorkshire, standing on the Cow and Calf rocks, as climbers puff and pull beneath him, and the moor stretches out behind while the landscape ripples in front, and on a clear day he swears he can see the North Sea. When the light is right. And I don't doubt he can see the waves, catching in the sun as they roll and break, even if I am standing there next to him and all I can see is a blur, where the land meets the sky.

At Stralsund, the passengers who have taken the ferry back to the mainland have disembarked now, and it is our turn to climb on board. In the sunshine, with the sound of the gulls and the rattling of the masts, the gentle thrum of the ferry engine ticking over in the background, the mood is good. I find a spot outside, on the back deck, and from the conversation around me it seems as if most on the boat are excited for their trip. There is something about islands that stirs the soul. They are alive with possibility, an endless source of fascination. Perhaps it is because they are contained, a world in and of themselves, surrounded by a natural border. They can be explored in their entirety, understood and mapped. I feel this too, and despite my reasons for this journey, I can share some of the excitement being felt all around me.

Yet I know there will be others on this boat. People who are travelling to the island with thoughts not of lazy summer days or walks along the beach, but people travelling home with their minds on bad exam marks or the cost of upcoming dental work, relationship concerns or dread for the future. And I share something with them too, the silent ones amidst the excited chatter of our fellow passengers. Silent, as if we know deep down that a ferry to an island on a sunny summer lunchtime should be a simple cause for joy and that despite our worries, we have no wish to bring down the mood.

*****

'My father's house,' Pascal says, 'is about half a kilometre from where my grandfather used to live. That house is now a second home for a couple from Hamburg, and whenever I've felt up to walking down the lane to take a look it has been shuttered and empty. There are still three options when you stand at my grandfather's old gate. You can head down the track towards town, as I used to do with him when we went for a walk together. You can go in the direction of the forest and path that leads to the lighthouse on the cliffs. Or you can follow a narrow, worn path that takes you through long grass and between the dunes until you've reached the very north end of the beach that stretches out for almost the entire length of the island on the seaward side.

Most people use that path to get down to the beach, but my mum would use it in order to follow the shore around the head of the island, clambering over the rocks as the land rose up beside her and she reached the foot of the cliffs. She would walk right round to the inland sea, picking her way through the big boulders and along narrow strips of sand. For some parts she had to take off her shoes and socks, rolling up her trousers to above the knee in order to paddle through the water. There are no real tides to speak of here, so she didn't need to worry about that as she went, but each year, when she did the walk for the first time, she would notice the things that had changed. Sandbanks that had appeared or been submerged. Parts of the cliffs that had crumbled and fallen. The flotsam and jetsam that had been caught between the rocks where the sea meets the land.

Most of these changes were the results of winter storms, when the waves ride high and the Baltic bathtub becomes a seething cauldron. Most of the things she found washed ashore were trash. Plastic containers and aluminium cans. Sometimes it was possible to still read the labels, and she could see if they came from Denmark or Sweden, West Germany or Poland. There were bits of rope, frayed at the ends, netting and plastic casings for who knows what. Sometimes she would find an old tin. For tobacco, perhaps. And she would drop it in the pocket of her long, yellow waterproof jacket that she always seemed to wear on her walks except for the very hottest of summer days.

I didn't go with her that often. I liked to walk with my grandfather, and the walk beneath the cliffs scared me. The sea on one side, however calm. The land, unstable and unclimbable on the other. There was a long, narrow stretch where the only possible movement was to continue forward or back, and it was easy to imagine the waters rising or the cliffs crumbling, of being caught or trapped with no way out. It's not that it wasn't possible, I remember my mum conceding once, but it was highly unlikely. After all, in the village I could be hit by a bicycle or choke on a bone from a fish roll. But still, I preferred the walk across the fields and up on top of the cliffs, and sometimes I would lean out as far as I dared and my grandfather would let me, to see if I could catch a glimpse of her yellow jacket, far below.

I never did, and I think that is why she liked that particular walk. For that stretch, as she rounded the head of the island to the point where the Baltic meets the lagoon, she was only really visible to someone out at sea. It was an escape, for an hour or two, from the outside world. Even on the island, it was always possible for the world beyond to intrude, brought ashore with the arrival of the next ferry.'

*****

The engines grow louder. Ropes are uncoiled. A crackle from the loudspeaker system and a cryptic instruction issued to a member of the crew. Movement.

*****

'I don't have any memory of my father joining us on our walks,' Pascal says, 'whether with my mum down below or with my grandfather, up on the cliffs. When we were on the island he used it as a time to write in peace, sitting in the small study room on the ground floor. It was easily the darkest room in the house, in the north corner of the building on the ground floor, close to the trees, but he liked it because it was cool in the summer and there was little view to distract him.

Once he felt as if he'd written enough, he would move around to the front of the house and the terrace, where it was possible to look right out across the fields, beyond the town and down to the ferry south of the island and the mainland beyond. We would find him there, reading or just looking. My mum would make the same joke about him taking a break and he would make the same reply, that in his head he was always working. Good answer, my mum would say, resting her hand on his knee as she sat down next to him.

Sometimes, in the evening, she would sing. One of my grandfather' friends, who lived a little further up the lane, would bring his guitar. There was a group back then, of people staying on the island, for whom the terrace of my grandfather's house was a magnet, a meeting point. And my mum would sing for them the songs she'd once sung in the backrooms of Berlin pubs, songs that she never forgot, even long after we'd moved to England. Some of them were her songs, but if she ever wrote them down we never found them, and my father and I can remember little more than fragments. Scraps of verses. A line from a chorus.

We could have waited a little longer... unspoken words that echo between us... please take the train, to the north country... hold me close as we walk through the pines... let us dream, dream of white horses...

*****

The city retreats, seeming to age as we get further away, the cars and scooters, the advertising signs and even the modern aquarium, fading into the background until all that is left are the red brick warehouses and the church towers behind, and it feels possible that I'm looking at the city as Pascal and his family saw it when they caught the ferry in the 1970s, or even what our predecessors experienced a century before.

*****

'And even if I can recall some of the words,' Pascal says. 'I don't know any of the tunes. I can't remember how the songs go.'

XXI.

On the ferry, the captain comes on to the loudspeaker. He tells us about the ferry that once carried railway carriages across to Rügen from the mainland. It was here, the captain says, that Lenin's sealed carriage was transported across the water on his way from Switzerland to Russia in 1917. A revolutionary journey. For a long time, the carriage was on display on Rügen, but it has been taken away now. The last he heard, it was in a train shed near Potsdam.

It is a story he has clearly told many times before, but it sounds like he still enjoys it.

*****

'During the last summer,' Pascal says, 'I was allowed to explore the island on my own. I had a bike there, one that had previously belonged to the son of my grandfather's neighbour, and he lent it to us so I could get around more easily. As long as I was home for the evening meal, and promised not to swim alone, I could go where I liked.

My favourite thing to do was to ride all the way down to the south end of the island, where it was possible to find spots, tucked away between dunes or with the right view of the mainland, where nothing man-made was in sight. No houses or pylons, no boats or cars. In those places I could play my game. I could pretend I was trapped on a desert island, collecting driftwood to make a shelter. Or else I pretended I was the last person alive after some terrible event. Of course, I didn't think about the fact that everything I could see was somehow shaped by humans. The fields and the forests. Even the white-crested waves, formed by breakwaters beneath the surface, a line-up of concrete blocks delivered by barge and dropped using a crane into the sea, all in the name of slowing the erosion of the shore.

Another place I liked to play was an old ruined building, also in the south, past the last of the villages and along a dirt track. It must have been about six or seven kilometres from the house, and it would take me about an hour to ride there, depending on what distracted me along the way. I knew nothing about the building, and had a sneaking suspicion that I probably wouldn't be allowed to play there if the adults knew about it, so I never asked. I invented stories and acted them out. One time it was a lookout point, in a war against some pirates. Another time it was a fisherman's hut, with a flat-bottomed sailing boat to work the waters of the inland sea moored outside. There were words scratched into the walls, most probably declarations of love by couples who had snuck in there for some privacy during a summertime romance, but I was too young to imagine such things, so instead I decided it must be some kind of code, the letters and numbers part of a message from the past to shadowy figures who would turn up at some point in the future.

I'd heard a radio show about ghosts, and how they might actually be imprints, stone-tape memories like photographic negatives, captured in the rock and reproduced when the atmospheric conditions were just right. This story, and the words scrawled on the wall, and the existence of the ruin itself, were all enough to convince me that this place would have tales to tell and that there must be some interesting scenes recorded in the brickwork. And so sometimes I would just sit there and wait, hoping the atmospheric conditions were in my favour, to catch a glimpse of the past.

There's no such thing as stone-tape memories of course, but part of me would still love it to be true. Because that would mean I could walk up to the old house and down the narrow path to the beach, following the shore round beneath the cliffs, to where the big rocks mark the boundary between the land and the sea, and if I waited for long enough, eventually my mum would appear again, if only for a fleeting glimpse, like the single remembered line of a song.'

*****

The straits have opened out now, the water slightly choppy as the wind blows across the inland sea. Off the back, Stralsund has retreated, a smudge of brown against the blue sky on the horizon. Off the front, the island has finally appeared, a thin sliver of gold where the sandbank curls around from the southern tip and the Baltic waters meet the lagoon. On either side of the ferry swans and eider ducks ride the rolling waves, and next to me a man rests his camera lens on the railing in an attempt to capture them, to take home a memory for a time when he is a long way from here.

*****

'My father woke me in the middle of the night,' Pascal says. 'I remember the feeling of being disorientated. I didn't know where I was at first. I thought we might be back in Berlin, that it was a dark, winter morning and I was late for school. But that wasn't it, my father told me, his voice gentle but insistent. We were still on the island. We were still at my grandfather's house. He wanted me to get up, because he didn't want me to miss what was happening.

I followed him out of the attic room, down the ladder to the landing, where the creak of the stairs in the quiet of the night sounded impossibly loud, but my father told me not to worry, that no one in the house was sleeping. My grandfather and mum were already outside, sitting on the terrace at the bottom of the front steps, wrapped in blankets.

Look, my father said, as we stepped outside. Down there.

From where we stood we could see right down the island, beyond the town and the villages, to the heath, glowing red and orange at the heart of the blackness all around. We would never find out how the fire started, and it was never reported on the news or in the papers. It happened in the part of the heath that back then was off limits, behind high fences where signs had been hammered into the heather warning of the consequences for those who might decide to trespass.

I had been down to the fence myself, a couple of times, where the island narrowed and only a small track between the dunes on one side and the fence at the edge of the heath on the other allowed access to the southern end of the island and my ruined building. Sometimes I stopped on the ride down to go up to the fence and see if I could find out what was on the other side, what might be happening in there. But I don't remember ever seeing a moving soul. Just an expanse of heather and drainage ditches dug a century or so before, and in the distance, where the heath met the inland sea, a collection of low, squat buildings that belonged to the navy.

I asked my grandfather, but he professed to know nothing. No big ships ever docked there, although sometimes we saw sleek, black speed boats racing south from the navy buildings across the lagoon towards the opening to the Baltic Sea. I later learned that there had been all kinds of rumours on the island, quietly shared, of military exercises and secret experiments, but nothing was ever confirmed, proven or disproven, even after all the files were opened. My father said we shouldn't be surprised. The biggest secrets would never come out. After all, they'd have been the first files into the shredder.'

*****

I look forward, across to the island. I'm trying to seek out a ruined building or the remains of a naval yard, the heather and sandbanks of Pascal's stories, his memories of the past meeting our present as the island draws ever nearer off the port bow.

*****

'After the fire there were more rumours,' Pascal says, 'especially once the explosions began. We were kilometres away, huddled up beneath the porch of my grandfather's house, but we still saw, heard and felt the bangs. A crack and then a low rumble, like an electric storm playing out right above our heads. Flashes of light in the distance. Vibrations through the wooden arms of the garden chair. A sabotaged weapons store or the heath giving up its secrets? Cold War supply malfunction or long forgotten munitions from forty years before? After the fire, on the island, I learned something about how our world worked then. Sometimes it was not about how a story was told, about official explanations or managed messages. Sometimes it was just about silence. And if nothing was ever said, how could we be sure that it really happened?

But I know that it did happen, because it is linked to one of my fondest memories of the island. Not the fire, or the explosions, because they were a little scary, even if my grandfather kept reassuring me about how far away it all was. No, it was the simple fact of being up in the middle of the night with the three of them, drinking hot tea, wrapped in those rough blankets while the adults sipped whisky. I can still taste the peppermint. I can see the glow of my mother's cigarette. I can smell the smoke from the fire as it drifted north. It was a still night. The fire burned itself out, although the next morning the heath was still smouldering. I was forbidden from taking my bike out to get a closer look. It was a day for playing in the garden, my grandfather said. When I finally made it down there, got close to the fence once more, the heath looked as it always had.

Silences. In the daylight, when I asked the adults again about what they thought had happened, there was no reply. But I saw the glances, exchanged across the breakfast table.

And then, about nine months later. Another night, waking in the attic. My father kneeling over me. It was a few days before we were to leave the island for the final time, at the end of that Easter holiday. I knew exactly where I was when I felt his presence. It was not a fire this time, he said, after I'd excitedly asked him. It was my mother. She wasn't in the house and they were worried about her. They needed to go out, to see if they could find her, but they didn't want to leave me alone. They didn't want me to wake up in an empty house.

So I went with them, my father and grandfather. We took torches and it was windy, the rain or spray from the sea, or a mix of both, wetting our hair and soaking our clothes. First we walked up the track through the forest, to the lighthouse and the cliffs. I can remember hurrying along, trying to keep pace with the long strides of the two men. I had never seen my father like this. Everything about him felt different, wrong somehow. It was in the way he walked, how he held his body. The look on his face. It was only later that I understood what it was, what he was experiencing. He was scared. I think that was the moment the sense of safety and security I'd always had as a child disappeared, the moment that I realised that there were some things my father couldn't control and make better. And then I was scared too. For us, but mostly for my mum.

After an hour or so walking the cliffs we had circled back to the house, and that was when I realised where she would be. We should have thought of it earlier, but something had driven the men to go high, up onto the cliffs. I only thought about it much later, what this might mean. What did they think they might find, when we went out into the storm? And why did they take me with them?

I led them down to the beach via the grassy path. The waves were crashing in now, a whipped up, churning mass of water that was so loud as it thrashed we could hardly hear each other as we called against the sound of the wind and the waves. We made our way to the north end of the beach and the rocks, slick and wet. We slipped and slithered our way around to beneath the cliffs, the waves breaking against our legs, until we found her. She was sitting at the bottom of a crack in the cliffs, sheltered from the storm on top of a large rock. The sandy walls rose up on either side, and above there was a tiny sliver of sky, stars appearing and disappearing at speed as the clouds raced across in front of them.

When we first saw her, my grandfather and father both stopped, waiting on the sand where the water foamed at their feet. I went over to her. She was wearing an old woollen jumper beneath her yellow jacket, and a pair of rubber boots. She smiled when she saw us. A tired smile, without surprise. I sensed she had been waiting for us. I climbed up onto the rock and she took me in her arms. It was late, she said. What was I doing up? I told her that we'd been looking for her. That the other two were worried about her. Was I not worried? I remember telling her no, I was not worried. She wouldn't have gone anywhere without us. That's right, she replied, and then slid forward, down off the rock and onto the sand.

I can still see the two indents left by her boots when she dropped down. As she walked towards the sea my grandfather had already turned towards home, but my father was staring at her. I couldn't read his face. There were emotions there that I had no access to. Perhaps I would understand better now. She took his hand and kissed him on the cheek, and then turned to reach out for me. As the waves continued to roll in we made our unsteady progress back towards the beach, following the agile figure of my grandfather as he led. I cannot hear the sea in this part of my memory, although the storm cannot possibly have stopped. The next sound I hear is the water boiling on the stove when we stepped into the kitchen, out of the wind, the whisky bottle waiting on the table.'

XXII.

It takes just over two hours for the ferry to reach the island from Stralsund, and I wonder how many trips the captain does each day. It's not a short journey, and the surroundings will change with the season and the weather, but I wonder if this is what he dreamed of as a young boy falling in love with the idea of the sea. Did he ever imagine that his ocean would be this lagoon? His Cape of Good Hope, the sandbanks at the southern tip of the island? Was he ever tempted to aim for the gap between the island and the mainland, and set course for the open waters of the Baltic?

For now, he is concentrating on his story as he steers the ferry up the channel. The island economy, he says, was once dominated by fishing. Later it became a popular destination for artists and writers, who came for the fresh air and the good light. Today, tourism is the most important industry, with fifty thousand guests coming for overnight stays and a quarter of a million daytrippers. There is some agriculture, he concedes, and on occasion the island has also been used as a location for film and television. Many families have been living on the island for generations, and for those of us planning on staying for a while, it surely wouldn't take us very long to learn their names.

*****

'If you walk up the track from my grandfather's house,' Pascal says, 'up towards the lighthouse, there's a spot by a bend where a gap opens up between the trees. You can see down to the water, and an inlet where the northern arm of the island curls around into the inland sea. From the lookout point you can also see a small island. There's not much there, just a couple of dead tree stumps and some large rocks. A few scraps of heather. We called it Cormorant Island because there were always black birds perched there, standing on the tree stumps between their fishing expeditions across the lagoon.

It wasn't just cormorants who gathered there, my grandfather used to say. It was also a meeting point for witches. They would stop over on the island on their way south each year to the slopes of the Brocken mountain. The Finnish witches and the Polish witches. The Swedish witches and the Danish witches. They would meet after travelling across the sea or along the coast, resting before their final journey for Walpurgis Night. It was the witches, my grandfather said, who had brought the stones. Any geologist would tell you that those stones should not be there. They were erratics, supposedly left behind with the retreat of the glaciers at the end of the last Ice Age. But it was impossible, or should have been, that so many could be gathered in one place. Not improbable, my grandfather said. Impossible. So it stood to reason that someone must have put them there, and on this he was sure. It was the witches.

One morning, during that last summer, as we walked up towards the lighthouse, at the point where the track curved round and the trees opened up, my grandfather pulled me to the side of the road. He wanted to show me something, he said. He led me through a tangle of bramble, under which it was possible to make out the faintest of tracks worn into the ground. It was a narrow path that hugged the hillside, snaking its way down with a series of sharp bends until it reached the water's edge.

It was a smugglers' path, my grandfather explained, his voice low. People used it to bring forbidden things onto the island under the cover of reeds below and the trees above. Years ago, for sure. Today? It was always possible. And it did feel like we were hidden from the world on that narrow path, only catching the occasional glimpse of the water as it got ever closer to us. We climbed over roots and small landslides, switchback after switchback, until we reached a muddy beach, right at the bottom.

We were talking in whispers now, my grandfather and I, even though there was surely no one around. He indicated that I should follow, and we walked on along the shore, where tall reeds grew higher than even my grandfather's head. After about five minutes of slow progress, we reached a fallen tree trunk where we sat down to rest.

Look, my grandfather said. Over there.

He pointed through the reeds to where a dark blue boat was moored, almost completely hidden. It was a family secret, he said. It had belonged to the house, tied up in the back and overgrown with weeds when they had first taken it over. One of the first things my grandfather did was to check it all over for holes and then take it down to the water. They used it occasionally, for little trips in the calm waters between the island and the mainland, until the directive came and all boats had to be registered. At that moment, he decided not to tell the authorities about it. Why, he couldn't say. So there it sat, floating in the shallows, hidden in the reeds. It was still in good condition, my grandfather said. It could still sail. And it was comforting to know that it was there.

The last time we were on the island, nine months later, it was only a week or so from Walpurgis Night. Couldn't we stay on a little longer, and see the witches when they arrived at Cormorant Island? My grandfather shook his head, and said that we had our own journey to make. And then he said that one day I would come back and take the boat over to the island to see the stones. I would be respectful. I wouldn't even land. I would leave everything as it was. He might not be around to join me, he said, but if he was, we would go together.

Of course, we never did. I asked my father about the boat, but he knew nothing of it. If it had been there, in the reeds, it would have been discovered long ago. In a strange way, he said, it was sometimes easier to hide things back then, when everyone thought everyone else was looking, keeping an eye out, than it would be today. A blue boat in the reeds would be discovered in a matter of days. Still, part of me thinks I should go down to the harbour and see if there is someone that would take me to the island. To see the stones. The other part of me thinks that it really doesn't matter. They won't have gone anywhere. It's enough to simply know they're there.'

*****

I think of Pascal in our house in Leeds. All his life in a rucksack. It was important to be able to up and leave. To hitch a ride. To catch a train. To get in the boat and sail away. The ferry is close to the island now, following the eastern shore up towards the town. I can see the sandbanks and a ruined building. Beyond, the purple fringe of heather. Here, the whole island sits low in the water, as if any kind of wave could take it under. My journey is almost over. I take out my phone to see if there are messages, but I've had no signal since the straits opened out into the inland sea and the eider ducks came alongside to say hello. It doesn't matter. They know I'm coming.

*****

'Two days after my mum's midnight walk,' Pascal says, 'we left the island for the final time. I remember standing on the terrace in front of the house, our bags at the bottom of the steps. Someone was coming from the harbour with a carriage to give us a lift to the ferry. My grandfather was cheerful, as if this was the same as all the other goodbyes. That we would be back soon. My mum was pale, steeling herself for the moment. My father was quiet. It was because of him that we were leaving. There was no blame attached to this, no judgement, but ultimately it was true. We all knew it, even me.

Behind the house the trees blew in the wind, and they seemed to be almost curling around the building as if to tell us not to worry, that the house and my grandfather would be protected even if we were many miles away.

The next time he saw me, my grandfather said, I'd be able to speak English. How do you do? Thank you very much! Have you met the Queen?

I can hear him saying these words, in a thick, almost parodic German accent. Yet I wonder if this can be true. My grandfather lived in London for years during the war. He spoke at least five languages fluently, and one of them was English. He still wrote letters to friends and, later, he would call us in Southport and insist on speaking English with me on the phone as I needed to practise and my parents would only teach me bad habits.

On that last morning on the island, I remember him taking my mother in his arms, speaking softly into her ear. The coast in England was beautiful, he said. She would soon see. And as for Wales and Scotland... it was hard for him to describe. And whenever she missed him she should just stand at the water's edge and know that there was nothing between them, just the wind and the waves that could carry one to the other.

I used to love the carriage journeys to and from the harbour, but not that day. My grandfather waved us off from the gate. He said he couldn't come to see us onto the ferry because he had some gardening to do, but I think it was just all too painful. I remember seeing my parents look at each other, and my mum take my father's hand, as she had done a few nights before at the bottom of the cliffs. She was telling him that it was going to be okay. That this was the right and only decision. That my grandfather understood. She said all these things without moving her lips, and of course I am only guessing, but I saw the tension leave my father's face in that moment, so even now, all these years later and as tired as I am, I don't think I am very far from the truth.'

*****

I get a signal as the ferry enters the harbour. No messages. I call up a map to make sure I know where I'm going. I turn Pascal's award over in my hand while the ropes are tied and the water churns as the ferry docks. Gulls hover above the quayside. Horse-drawn carriages and electric golf carts are waiting to take visitors to their hotels or holiday apartments. The restaurant terraces around the harbour are full, the sound of conversation and the chink of cutlery on china. It's mid-afternoon, but on the island there is plenty of time to linger over lunch.

Welcome, the captain says, his final moment at the microphone before we disembark. He hopes we'll have a wonderful time in this truly special place.

*****

'The first few weeks in England were hard,' Pascal says. 'But we found our feet. Perhaps we are indeed a family of exiles. Perhaps it's true that there's something in us that means we know how to start again. Lessons learned and passed on. It's not special, I suppose. There are millions and millions who have done it. Increasingly I think it is the people who have stayed put who are the anomaly. The families on this island who can trace their history back generations. It's a story the ferry captain likes to tell, and he presents it as a positive, but I can't help thinking there's something sad about it too.

In England, the house really helped. Close to the beach and the sea. You could smell it, drifting in through the kitchen window. You could hear the gulls above the estate. We had the weekend walks through the dunes and onto the beach, where the sand seemed to stretch away to the very horizon. If the weather was right, the air clear with no haze, you could see Blackpool Tower in one direction and the Welsh mountains in the other.

To be truthful, though, I don't think my mother had much attention for these landmarks, or the oil rigs and the tankers out on the Irish Sea. She barely noticed the dogs racing across the

162

damp sands, the kites bobbing and weaving above our heads, or the grand, water-stained houses that looked out to the beach from the other side of the dunes. She would take her shoes off and close her eyes. If she did that, she said, she could be back under those cliffs again, just for a moment. And if she could return to the island from the sands of the Irish Sea, then it would never really leave her. It would never be truly far away.'

*****

I stand on the quayside holding Pascal's award. It shines in the sun. Everything is soft. The wind against my skin. The sun. My vision. My brain. Pascal is still talking to me. Pascal is waiting for me. I check the map one more time, adjust my bag on my shoulder, and then I start to walk.

*****

'The island is the place,' Pascal says. 'I know it now. All that time when I didn't come back, I thought it would be too painful. To see the house and to feel the memories. It could only remind me of what I'd lost. But it hasn't been like that, Ben. It hasn't been like that at all. I only wish now that I'd brought more people here. I wish that I could have walked the beach with Anna, taken her around the head of the island, under the cliffs. I see her face, and the faces of others too. The ones I would have liked to bring here, only I didn't know it at the time.

The island is the place. The reason I refused to return is also the reason why it is so. People. Memories. Love. Here I can find them again. We were all here, Ben. And soon you will be too.'

XXIII.

The last photograph Pascal sent to me was never printed out. I didn't add it to the list. I think of it now as I walk, through the town and the crowds of people dawdling in the warm afternoon sun. It was two weeks ago that he sent it, along with the message that he wouldn't make it to London. As soon as I saw where he was, he wrote, I would understand.

The photograph was of a hospital room. I could tell from the bed and from the floor, but otherwise there was very little medical equipment in view. A small bedside table with a pot of flowers and a book, open and placed face down. A wardrobe, the door ajar, and a single shirt hanging from the rail. Through the window I could see trees, the branches brushing up against the glass. The hospital room was above the ground floor. There was a chance it had a view.

'I lay in that bed,' Pascal says, 'and all I could think was that I was not going to end up here. That this was not to be the last room. They told me that there was no need for me to stay, but that they could make me more comfortable. If I insisted, and my father was willing, I could of course return to the island. I looked over to him and he just nodded. We spoke no words about it, but I knew what he was thinking. He was thinking of mum, and how we never got to take her home, even for just one more night. For one more view of the dunes.

He was determined that this was not how my story would end, and I found that I was determined too. The ferry journey back was rough. The inland sea choppy and the captain concentrated. There was no time for stories on this voyage. I was sick, and I never get sick. I told the crew member who just looked like he'd heard it all before. But I insisted. I never get sick! I don't know why it was so important to me, why I felt I had to tell him, again and again, even as I could feel the vomit building in my throat as the boat moved beneath me.

From inside the toilet cubicle I could hear my father talking in a low voice, and when I came back out the crew member had nothing but concern in his eyes and that look on his face that I've learned to recognise, when people don't know what to say. Some try to fill the silence with touch, as he did, patting me gently on the shoulder. I didn't mind.

Yes, the ferry back to the island was rough, but I was determined. There are many worse places than that room on the fourth floor of the hospital, with its view across the gardens and a huge expanse of sky. But I wanted to go home. That's what I told the nurse, and I was surprised as I said it. She looked at me as if she understood, but she couldn't, not really, because I didn't understand myself. Until then I'd never thought of this house, of the island, as home. I didn't think home existed. And yet here I am.'

*****

I walk through town past the souvenir shops and ice cream stalls, the summer theatre and the thatched cottages that have long been converted into holiday rentals. I reach the track that turns north, concrete slab laid next to concrete slab, marking its route across to where the land rises up, with the fields running away to the inland sea on one side and the dunes on the other. The wind is warm, blowing in from the south, and when I clamber up onto the dunes I can see the waves racing almost parallel to the beach, curling and breaking, rising up and diving down, a swirling, churning dance.

At Pascal's father's house I stop at the gate. I recognised it from a distance, from the descriptions Pascal sent to me. Red brick with two storeys, the second under a thatched roof. It looks old but it's new, like so much on the island. The garden is surrounded by a fence against which rosehip bushes grow, blocking the view of all but the most curious of passers-by to a garden containing nothing but a neat lawn and a gravel path between the front door and the gate. Trees grow on either side of the house and from a distance it was possible to get a sense of the size of the garden, running out from the back and down towards the dunes and the beach beyond.

I push open the gate and hear myself walking down the path, footstep after footstep. Instinctively I attempt to be lighter on my feet, to make less noise as I walk up to the front door, but there is no-one in the house to disturb. I don't know how I know it, but I do, even in my exhausted state. I recognised it from a distance, as I first recognised the house with its red bricks and thatched roof. I knew it was empty. That Pascal's father had called me and I had come as quickly as I could, but that I'm too late.

My right hand drops from where I pressed the bell. My bag is at my feet. In my left hand, I hold Pascal's award. I turn it over and the sun shines off its edges. Behind me the island stretches away to the south, hazy in the distance. Above the fields beyond the front gate and the concrete-slab track, a buzzard hovers above where horses graze, some taking shelter by the water trough in the shade of a huge, solitary oak tree.

*****

'At what point in your life do you think about where you would like to end up?' Pascal said. 'I don't think my father ever thought of it for himself until mum died, but after that he was always very clear. Even before the Wall came down he talked of the island, dreamed of coming back here. It was here that she was the most happy, he said. It was here that she returned to, in her memory and when she closed her eyes on the beach in Southport. Do you know, Ben? Do you know where you want to end up? Do you have your own island of the imagination? What do you dream of, when I dream of white horses?'

*****

I sit on the step for almost two hours, watching dusk approach, and then, with the light fading, I see a figure in the distance, coming down the lane. He walks slowly, but with purpose, hunched slightly but with strong steps. As he pushes open the gate he takes his hat off, and then looks me directly in the eyes. They are dry, but I can tell they haven't been.

'Ben,' he says. 'It's wonderful to meet you at last.'

I step forward and almost fall into his arms. We embrace on the gravel path, each holding the other with an intensity that makes it clear that in our hearts that we are holding someone else.

We step back and stand, facing each other. He is still holding my shoulders. He asks me if I would accompany him for a walk. He knows it is going dark, but he is not ready to return to the house quite yet. Would I keep him company? I am to call him Alexander, he says, and I must stay the night, as planned, and for as long as I want.

'Pascal spoke a lot about you in the past few weeks,' Alexander says. 'He would say *I need to speak to Ben* and I would hear his voice from behind the closed door of his room, making his recordings. Sometimes he would ask me questions about a certain memory or story, and quite often he was annoyed with my answer. I presume it was because sometimes I remembered things differently. So then he stopped asking me, which was his right. And I suppose, in a way, he was correct. These are his memories. They are his truth.'

We follow a path up to a small settlement at the bottom of the hill, the forest coming down to meet the houses. The first lights are coming on, above the porches and on the corner where a street lamp stands beside the bus stop. We must be close to Pascal's grandfather's house, but Alexander doesn't point it out. Instead he shows me the house of a famous writer, now a museum. I ask him if one day they will turn his house into a museum and he turns to look at me and, after a moment's hesitation, begins to laugh.

'It was quiet in the end,' Alexander says. 'He knew it was time. We spoke no more words. The doctor was there, but he stepped out of the room. It was just the two of us. His breath weakened and I felt the grip on my hand loosen; there was a bird in the garden singing as I told him I loved him. In the background was the sound of the sea, and then he was gone, and the waves continued to roll in and the bird continued to sing.'

At a crossroads the track, now made up of dusty, compressed earth, is covered in piles of horse manure from the delivery wagons and tourist carriages lined up in a clearing beneath the trees.

'It sounds peaceful,' Alexander says, 'But I know it wasn't. Not inside. He was fighting for every minute. He was in pain and he was pained. He hated that this had happened to him. He railed against it. It was *fucking shit*, he said, in English, over and over again. *Fucking shit fucking shit fuck...* He was trying to express his sense that it just wasn't fair. And then he would stop, take a breath, and go up to his room and talk to you. He was resolved. He couldn't be upset all the time. He had work to do.'

The path leads up towards the lighthouse, directions on a little green sign, still visible in the gloaming. The trees open out by a bend in the road and there's a view down to an inlet and an island of stunted trees and shadowy rocks. I've stopped but Alexander has kept walking, his stride long. I don't want to run after him so I take my time to catch him up,. We come together once more after two further bends in the track, as it snakes up the hillside to where the lighthouse shines out its warning.

'Would it be possible to hear Pascal's recordings,' Alexander says. 'Not immediately. But in the future? I think I would like to listen to his stories. To hear his memories. To hear his voice. Do you think?'

At the lighthouse we look out to the west, across the Baltic Sea that has grown calmer now, the choppy waves replaced with a rolling swell, nothing breaking on the surface except the occasional cormorant flying low across the water, making a dive for fish. The sun has almost dropped completely beyond the horizon. The lighthouse casts a long shadow.

'You must be exhausted,' Alexander says. 'We should get something to eat.'

I am beyond hunger and tiredness. I know I should be more tired, more hungry and more upset. But I am beyond it all. Alexander turns on his heel and I follow, back down the track until we reach the crossroads where the horses and carriages wait, and there's a small restaurant and beer garden. It's quiet. Most of the daytrippers have left the island. We order beers and, when they arrive, we toast our loss.

*****

'I remember,' Alexander says, 'when Pascal was born. There was this intense few hours. Perhaps it was longer. I couldn't reach the hospital, and I thought I was going to be late. And then of course there was the birth, which was not without complications, and afterwards they told us that Pascal and Clara would have to stay in hospital for about a week. It was nothing serious, just a precaution, but they wanted to keep an eye on both of them. I was to go home and rest because, when they did come home, I was going to have to do everything for them. And the nurses laughed at this. They were greatly amused by the idea.

So having thought I'd be leaving the hospital with my wife and our son, to take him back to the apartment where we'd painted a corner of the bedroom with a rainbow and stars, where there was a crib with a mobile hanging over it, and three neat piles of cloth nappies and everything else we needed, I stepped out onto the street empty handed, and nearly got hit by a tram because I was in such a daze.

I remember walking home, past where the demonstration had been earlier in the day, the one that blocked my way to the hospital, and the banners and flags were still hanging from the buildings on either side of the street but the cars were moving again and there was no one in uniform in sight. I walked home but then continued on, past the apartment, through Prenzlauer Berg and up into Pankow, around to Weißensee, and then eventually I was almost back at the hospital again. The whole while I wasn't thinking about anything. I wasn't thinking about Clara or Pascal, who didn't even have a name yet. I wasn't thinking about my work or my friends or anything else. It was like there'd been this build up, weeks and months of preparing, of getting ready, of waiting for this day to come with antici-pation and not a little fear, and then it was here and there was nothing left. I was drained. Empty.

I was on a little side street in Weißensee, close to the hospital where I presumed both Clara and Pascal lay sleeping. I stepped into a tiny pub where everyone was smoking between sips of beer and *korn* and I decided to have a drink. I spoke to nobody, but just slowly drank my beer and then ordered another. And I slowly drank that one and ordered another, and the feeling was strange because there was no pain to numb or joy to accentuate, just that emptiness to fill, and I could tell, even by the end of the second beer, that it wasn't going to work. Still, I kept ordering. A third, a fourth. A fifth. And then I went home and slept for about twelve hours.'

*****

On the other side of the restaurant, a man wearing an old sailor's hat begins to play the accordion. A woman sitting at the table next to us gives a spontaneous clap of what can only be excitement. The island is clearly everything she'd hoped it would be.

*****

'I haven't experienced that feeling again,' Alexander says, 'until today. I was walking home from the doctor's surgery. We had taken Pascal there, ready to be picked up by the undertaker. He has to come over from the mainland, but the doctor told me not to worry. He has his own boat.'

Alexander looks over to the waiter and catches his eye. Orders another.

XXIV.

It is dark when we walk back to the house, following the track past the writer's house to the dunes and the fields. My bag is still sitting on the step where I left it, underneath a small table by the door where I placed Pascal's award. Alexander picks it up and turns it over in his hand, smiles, and carries it in with him.

Inside the house, we walk through to the kitchen, with its view into the dark garden. There is little clutter in the house, no papers on the sideboard or on the counter, no books left lying around. Everything is neat and orderly, in and of its place. The only thing that hasn't been tidied away is a slim book on top of a padded envelope on the kitchen table. Alexander takes it, and passes it to me.

It is a collection of short stories. The first he has published in nearly forty years. Inside, it is dedicated to Pascal. He tells me I can take it. I thank him and then, after a moment's pause, I admit that I've hardly read anything he's written, even though Sara is a big fan.

Alexander laughs. A big, loud laugh, from deep inside him, and then offers me a whisky.

In the living room in Leeds. A bottle of whisky and a bottle of cola. A bag of ice in the freezer, picked up from the late night garage at the top of the road. In the morning, when the sun comes up, we will walk into town. For now there's a football match, a UEFA Cup semi final against Barcelona, and then a film from the video shop on the corner. At half-time Pascal tells me of his plans. He wants to be the greatest photographer who ever lived. It is the bravado of bourbon and coke. He wants to be Henri Cartier-Bresson. He wants to be Inge Morath. What did I say? Who did I want to be? Did I name the great writers? Or had I already stopped believing? What were we dreaming of on Richmond Mount? And did we get there?

We sit in silence on the terrace. All the lights in the house are out and we are left with the moon and the stars. Pascal's room is right above where I'm sitting. This was his view. Tomorrow morning, when the light is right, I will do what he asked me to do and take what will be the final photograph. A room with a view across the dunes.

In Landeck, we meet by the river and then walk up to the castle. Sara stays at the campsite, two valleys over and I drive to meet him. She hurt her ankle on a walk the day before and she needs to let it rest. Naturally, Pascal comes on the train, from Innsbruck where he has some photographs in a small exhibition. The mountains around are shrouded in mist, and a light drizzle falls. Pascal has heard that there's a restaurant up at the castle, with great views of the mountain from the terrace, but when we get to the top of the hill the restaurant is closed.

Ruhetag. Day of Rest.

On the walk up I tell him Sara and I are planning to get married. We sit on the low wall by the castle car park and he asks me if this is it. Will I be staying in Germany forever? In Berlin?

I cannot remember what I answered.

Sara dreams of a house by the lake. What did Anna dream of, on that roof terrace in London? Sara wants to feel the warmth of the south on her face. Pascal said they almost made it. Would Anna be here now? I want to be where Sara is. We never know where we're going to end up.

*****

'We do not finish with the hospital room,' Pascal said. 'The final room will be this one, and I will leave it for you to take the picture. If nothing else, it means you have to come. You have to come to the island and come to the house. You have to stand here and see what it is that I see. The place where it's going to end.

Since I arrived here, on the days when I've had enough energy, I've walked with my father down to the beach or up into the forest. One day we took a carriage down to the bottom of the island. I wasn't in search of memories, and we didn't talk of the past. I have you for that.

What I wanted was to create a new memory, so that for a little while longer we didn't have to live only in the past. Should we go out for dinner tomorrow? Something to look forward to, however small. On the carriage ride we spoke about him and his work, and my hopes for his writing and how the world was going to discover him again. He'd just been told that one of his plays is to be performed in Vienna. And the book is about to come out.

I still don't know if he stopped writing all those years, and I don't want to ask him. He will decide what he wants people to read when he's ready. When he feels like he has something he wants to say and that he wants people to hear. When he told me he was finished, I was pleased, but I told him that I hoped he hadn't rushed them for me. I was joking, but he answered me seriously.

It was possible, he said.

I read all the stories. He wanted to wait until the book was finished, properly bound and published, but we were worried about how much time was left. So he brought the proofs to me when they arrived by post from Berlin, and I laid them all out on the bed. Reading has been getting harder, so it took me a while. One story a day, until they were finished. They aren't exactly long, but still, one a day was about all I could manage.

In most of the stories I recognised nothing. They belonged to different times and places, the periods I have no knowledge of or the parts of my father's imagination I have no access to. But there were some things I recognised, some parts that I knew. I knew the places he was describing and versions of the people. And in those stories I read about my father and my mother. I read about me. They're good stories and it's a good book. But, I told him, he'll write better. There's still time.'

*****

Into the silence and the moonlight I tell Alexander how happy Pascal was to be here. How it comes through in the recordings, and that when he listens to them he will hear it for himself. He will see what the island meant to Pascal, and that it had less to do with the place itself and more to do with the people, those who had been with him here in the past and who were with him here at the end.

Alexander listens, turning the whisky glass in his hand.

The wind has picked up slightly. Beside the house, the trees creak. At the bottom of the garden, the reeds whisper, but we cannot make out what they are saying.

Alexander stands and moves past me, into the house, pausing for a second by my side to rest his hand on my shoulder. And then he's gone, leaving me to the sound of the wind as it blows across the garden, leaving me to the stars and the sea. If I close my eyes I can hear the reeds and I can hear the waves, breaking gently on the sands where a family used to walk, and I can hear Pascal speaking to me as he has done from those long nights in a Leeds living room to the very recent past, all the way from London to the island, and when I hear him, I hear a voice so strong and clear, and so alive.

Acknowledgements

The title of this book comes from a famous rock climb at Gogarth at the north end of Holy Island/Ynys Gybi, itself just off the coast of Anglesey/Ynys Môn in North Wales. The first ascent of 'A Dream of White Horses' was by Ed Drummond and Dave Pearce in 1968, and although it has always been a climb way beyond my modest abilities, there is something about the name that has stayed with me since I first heard it during our summer camping trips to Rhoscolyn at the south end of the same island in the 1980s. More than anything, it seemed to explain perfectly how I felt about this special place when I was away from it and my longing to return. It still does to this day.

Many thanks to Kevin and Hetha Duffy and everyone at Bluemoose Books for believing in this book and my writing. Thanks to Fiachra McCarthy for the cover design. Special thanks to my editor Leonora Rustamova for her insight, input and enthusiasm. It's been a joy to work together.

Thanks to Sarah for conversations in Berlin in the early days of this project, to my family and friends for all their support, and to those of you who shared the days of Raven Road when everything was in front of us and we had no idea what was coming next.

Thanks to Katrin and Lotte for your love and joy and for the excitement of exploring the world together.

And finally, to Tom: thanks for your friendship. It means everything.